P9-EEP-585

PLEASANTON
CITY OF PLANNED PROGRESS
Inc. 1894

You Can Call Me Worm

You Can Call Me Worm

Dan Haas

Houghton Mifflin Company · Boston · 1997

For information about this and other Houghton Mifflin trade
and reference books and multimedia products, visit
The Bookstore at Houghton Mifflin on the World Wide Web
at http://www.hmco.com/trade/.

The text of this book is set in 12.5 point Janson Text.

Library of Congress Cataloging-in-Publication Data
Haas, Dan.
You can call me Worm / by Dan Haas.
p. cm.
Summary: Hoping to help their troubled father,
who has been sitting on his roof for several days,
Worm and his older brother set out from their mother's
house on a trek across suburban Virginia.
ISBN 0-395-85783-X
[1. Brothers — Fiction. 2. Fathers and sons — Fiction.
3. Divorce — Fiction. 4. Depression, Mental — Fiction.] I. Title.
PZ7.H1123115Yo 1997 97-6466
[Fic] — dc21 CIP AC

Manufactured in the United States of America
BP 10 9 8 7 6 5 4 3 2 1

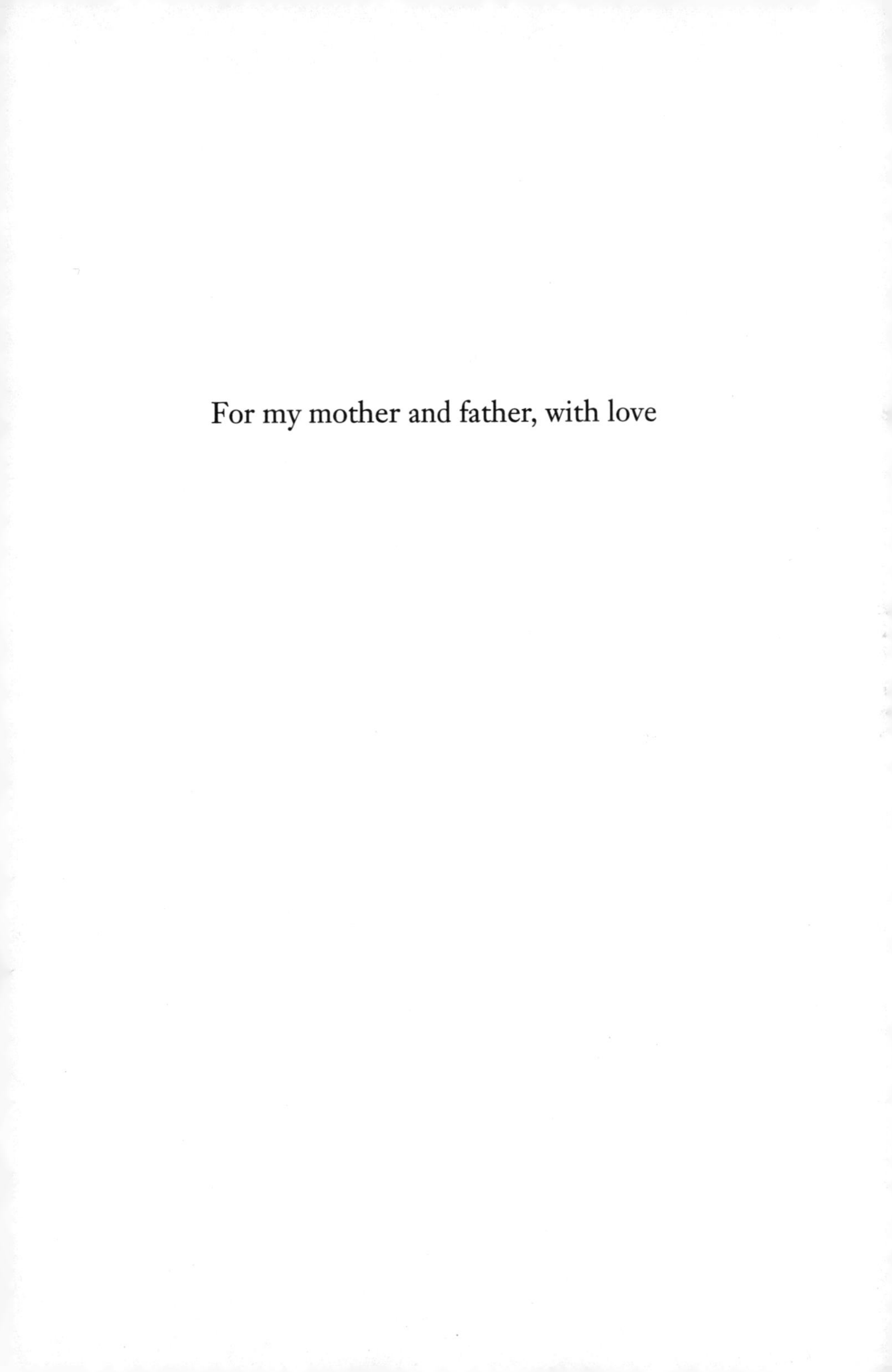

For my mother and father, with love

You Can Call Me Worm

ONE

I found out at school that my father had been sitting on the roof of his house for two days. Danny Zinkus and Chris Kelly told me in the locker room, right before gym class.

"Hey, Worm," they said, "What's your old man's last name?"

"Same as mine, you seropurulent eighth graders." (Luckily, I'd just been in the library checking the dictionary for quality insults for people like Zinkus and Kelly.)

"Thought so," said Zinkus. "He lives over by Fort Wilson, right? Did you know he's gone nuts? My cousin over there, he says your old man's been sitting on his roof for two days and doesn't want to come down."

I wanted to come back at those two stuck-up, pimple-faced eighth graders with an even more powerful insult, but I had a problem.

This sounded just like Dad.

Not that he's ever sat on a roof for two days before. But one of his favorite trips he used to do with my brother Todd and me was to go to this hill above the Beltway. (The Beltway is a highway that goes around and around Washington, DC, through the suburbs where we live.) On a Saturday morning when the weather was nice, or even if it wasn't so nice, we'd all three pack a lunch and just go and sit on that hill and watch the cars go by. I realize it sounds boring, but it never was. There was something about sitting up there watching all those people cruise by and knowing that they couldn't see you, and feeling lucky because you got to lie back in the sweet grass while they had to drive to wherever, and you didn't have anything in the entire world to do, not even a hike to finish or a pool to swim across. I just all out loved it. We'd all talk like we were just the same age, none of this "Oh here comes Worm" stuff that I always get in school because I'm young for my grade and I act goofy. We'd just talk about anything, even girls that Todd wanted to go out with but was afraid to ask. It was so cool to know that Todd was actually afraid of something.

When Dad was younger, before he and Mom had us, his idea of a good time was to go off into the woods all by himself for a week and live on canned beans and just sit and watch for animals to come by. Once when I was little he spent most of his vacation trying to learn how to stand on his head and how to snap his fingers. He said he was worried that if he didn't focus on those things, and learn them, that he might go through his entire life without ever knowing how to stand on his head or snap his fingers. It seemed to me like a completely normal and sensible way to spend your vacation, and that's the way it's always been with my dad. The stuff that he does seems normal to me.

But ever since he and Mom broke up (if I'm going to be really honest), I'd have to say I have been worried about him. It's been sixteen months plus two weeks now, and at the start we saw him every weekend. But now he has that little house over by Fort Wilson, and he says he's really busy looking for a job (he lost his old one right before they broke up) and even when he does come and get us for a weekend, it's not the way it used to be. Like one time he took us to the boat basin at Lake Accomack, which, don't get me wrong, is an OK place to go on a Saturday, but it's not the kind of place Dad used to take us. It used to be we'd just drive around until we found some woods that looked interesting and then just park and go stomping right in there and sometimes find out we were on somebody's private property and get kicked off, or else go to an open house at one of these really expensive new homes bigger than barns and pretend we really wanted to buy it and go into the bathroom and criticize the faucets. Just really fun stuff. Once we drove to West Virginia because Dad had to see some movie, and it turned out to be *Godzilla Meets Mothra*. I couldn't figure out why, now that he was divorced, he was taking us to feed the ducks and go on a paddle-boat ride at Lake Accomack. Did he think he now had to be an officially Normal Father? But I was sort of afraid to ask him. He started feeding the ducks, but right after he started someone else came along with duck food and the whole flock went over to the new person. But Dad just kept crouching there, tossing out duck food that just hit the ground and stayed there. And when he'd run out of duck food, he just kept on crouching there.

Until finally Todd called, "Hey, Dad. Want to go on a paddle-boat?" Then Dad got up, and we went on the paddle-boat. We went across the lake and back, but no one said anything, and he took us back to Mom's right on time.

So when I heard he was sitting on a roof, I found Todd as soon as I could. He was outside, fortunately, in another gym class, and I was playing right field in our softball game, so that allowed me to sort of sneak over to the edge of the ditch and call across to Todd, who was with his friends doing hurdles. I said, "Zinkus and Kelly say Dad's sitting on his roof."

Todd put a hand in the face of the other guy who was trying to talk to him, looked at me for a minute, and said, "Tell them, after school. At the Chair."

I nodded, ran back to right field, and Mr. Harris never even noticed I'd been gone. Hardly anyone hit the ball to right field anyway; that's why I was there.

The Chair was actually a place. It was in the woods not too far from our house. Somebody, nobody really remembered who, had dragged an old chair out there to a clearing and now it was a place where the older kids met to smoke and where we little kids would hang out if the high-school kids weren't there. Todd was now a high-school kid, being in ninth grade, and one way you knew that he had a lot of respect (considering he was a ninth grader) was that nobody ever told him to get lost when he went to the Chair.

When we got there, Zinkus and Kelly were already waiting for us.

"Tell me what you told Worm," he said to them.

"Worm, did you run and tell your big brother what we said?" said Zinkus.

"Worm, did we worry you?" said Kelly.

Maybe I should explain something here.

My name is Will Glasser. The reason everyone

except my parents call me Worm is that I once ate a worm, when I was seven years old. We were outside, all my friends and I, and someone dared me to do it, and I wanted to prove my courage, so I proved it, and I've been sorry ever since. That name just stuck, and I'm not sure why.

I'm lying about that.

I'll tell you the reason it stuck: I'm the sort of person who it's easy for people to call Worm. Why? Because I put different-colored socks on in the morning and don't even notice it. Because if I go off to the woods with my friends to build a tree fort, I'm the one who falls off the first board we nail up and hang off it by my hands until I fall in the creek and everybody cracks up, so I spend the rest of the time watching everyone else build it because they say I make them nervous if I'm up in the tree. Because if the instructions on a box of brownie mix say "Beat by hand," I'm the one who sticks his hands right into the bowl and beats it by hand until my hands are all covered with brownie mix and my big brother comes into the kitchen and laughs so hard he falls over. Because this kind of thing happens all the time, and I can't help it, and so I get nervous around people and tell stupid jokes that make them absolutely certain that I'm a moron. So everyone except my parents calls me Worm, even my best friends Ken and Robert, and once in a while even Mom will, because sometimes she thinks it's cute.

But Dad never does. He figured out how I really feel about it, even though I never tell anyone, and that's another reason why I missed him so much.

"AAAAAAAAAAAW," said Zinkus, and actually put his hand on my shoulder. "It'll be OK, Worm."

Seropurulent: (adjective) Consisting of serum and pus.

"Tell me what you told Worm," Todd said again, and Zinkus said, "We just told him what we heard from one of our cousins. Everyone in their neighborhood over there is talking about it. Your old man's been sitting on his roof for two days. I think my cousin said they even called the police, and the police said it wasn't any of their business if somebody wanted to sit on his roof."

"It's not against the law," I said, but nobody paid attention.

"Two days?" Todd said.

"I told you," said Zinkus. He held up two fingers and said it again, "Two days."

"Two days," Todd said, as if this had some deep inner meaning, and he turned around and started to walk away. He was getting to be so cool he didn't even have to say goodbye anymore. So I said it: "Farewell, oh abhorrent eighth graders!"

"Beat it, Worm."

I hurried after Todd. The woods had that baked smell they get in the summertime, at the end of a ninety-nine–degree day. The dead leaves, the live leaves on the trees, the honeysuckle, even the water in the little creek there, everything smelled like it was just about to start rotting from the heat. Where we live, on days like that, you pray for a thunderstorm at the end of the day and you usually get it. My prayer was answered before Todd and I got home, though, and we had to run the last block with the rain hitting so hard it made little spray explosions on the street. I know we were both thinking about Dad, and if he was up on that roof getting soaked.

Ever since the breakup, Mom almost always got home before we did. She'd worked out some deal with her boss. It was nice, but sometimes we felt like she was being almost too nice to us. Sometimes I wanted to say, "It's OK, Mom. We're big boys. We'll survive." But sometimes I was so glad she was there when we got home that I just wanted to cuddle up with her in front of the TV, with me drinking Ovaltine and her drinking flat soda from the night before (her favorite drink, I'm not kidding). In fact, sometimes we did cuddle up in front of the TV and watch *Sesame Street.* But I was always scared Ken would come over and see me.

Today she was being extra nice. Even though it was only Wednesday, we were going out to Pizza Hut. "What's the occasion?" Todd asked, and Mom said, "No occasion. That's the whole point. We're going to celebrate a perfectly ordinary normal Wednesday."

It was a nice idea, but Todd and I weren't in the mood to be grateful and cheerful that night. He grabbed me as we were walking outside and whispered into my ear, real hot and loud, "*Don't* tell her about Dad!" I wondered why not, and couldn't think why, and that gave me something else to be quiet about when we got to the restaurant.

Mom wanted to have a nice conversation and spend some quality time with us. She knew better than to ask us about school, so she asked Todd how he thought the track team would do next year, a subject dear to his heart since he's the star hurdler. But even he wasn't trying, tonight. And he's Mom's favorite. I know I'm not supposed to say that because there aren't supposed to be favorites in families, but it was true. She smiled differently for him. "OK, I guess," he said, and he sipped his water. He's so healthy now he doesn't even drink Coke.

I was drinking root beer. And I at least tried, when Mom asked me about what I was reading these days.

"A horror story," I said.

"What's it about?"

"A werewolf."

"Sounds suspenseful."

"It is."

"I'm reading a kind of mystery set in a convent."

"Good."

"I think you're supposed to think the murderer is a nun, but I've already figured out who it is."

"Great."

"I think it's the handyman."

"Probably."

"So Todd — how do you think the football team will do?

Well, maybe I wasn't trying that hard either.

I should tell you something else. A couple of nights before this, Mom had announced that we weren't going to be seeing Dad at all for a while. That she couldn't exactly tell us why, but just that he'd been having a difficult time lately, and she didn't think it would be a good idea for a while. And Todd tore into her. It was pretty awful. He said she was trying to keep us away from him, and she said he didn't understand, and by the end they were both crying in their own rooms. The night after that she told us it was because Dad had called her up, just off-the-wall angry, a way she'd never heard him before, and she was just scared and she wanted us to be away from him for a while, just for a while. But since they disconnected Dad's phone for some reason, we were totally cut off from him. And Todd still blamed Mom. This made it a little harder to be cheerful at Pizza Hut.

I was tired of thinking about Dad, to tell you the

truth, so I watched Mom trying to talk to Todd, and I wondered why she and Dad had gotten married. She was beautiful — that was one reason he'd married her, I knew. She's very small, and she has this beautiful curly brown hair, and she's in really good shape, always has been, and she has the biggest eyes I think I've ever seen on anyone. I knew another reason why Dad married her: the way she listens to you with those eyes. She soaks up every word you're saying. And Dad needed a person who could keep his life organized. Mom is sure excellent at that. But why did she marry him? Because he was funny? Because he was smart? Because he could open a soda bottle with his teeth?

All they ever used to argue about was the news. I'm serious, every night they'd be yelling about something the President said, and I'd think: He lives in the White House, guys. You don't even know him. He doesn't give two flying diddlies about you. They'd scream at each other every night about the President or something that happened in Africa or something about the stock market and next thing you know it's: "Boys, I have to tell you, your father and I are separating." Why? "We just have to choose between our marriage and keeping our own selves together." What does *that* mean? "I'll be able to explain it better when you're older." Knowing they were splitting up sure made me feel old enough to know why. But we were eating dinner when she told us and she started to cry and this big tear slid down her nose and plopped into her soda. And then I realized I was crying too. So I just ran up to my room.

The pizza came and helped me stop wondering about all that, and I also quit wondering why Todd had so much hair in his nose. See, whenever I'm thinking about something serious, I always think about something stupid at the same time. The truth is, I'm always thinking about something stupid, like how the world can be divided into people who like the smell of gasoline and people who don't, or whether you could suffer intestinal injuries from lighting a fart, or why God gave boys nipples. Only once in a while do I think about something serious.

A couple of trips to Pizza Hut ago, I'd told Mom I no longer liked pepperonis. Too salty. They made me want to drink a gallon of water. But she'd forgotten, and there I was, face to face with a pepperoni pizza and a mother smiling because she thought she'd gotten me my favorite. So I had no choice but to chow down the pepperoni pizza, but I must not have looked that enthusiastic. Mom didn't even try talking to me. She and Todd droned on about something, and I started wondering what the big deal was with not telling Mom about Dad and the roof, and then I decided I shouldn't space out that obviously, and I took a big gulp of root beer and smiled at Mom and said, "How come boys have nipples?" And she threw down her napkin and said, "Let's go.

Are you finished? Let's go. Next time I try to do something nice, remind me not to!"

Todd told me later she'd been trying to ask me about school for about three minutes, but I'd been so off on another planet that I never answered. Until I came up with my big question.

Typical, I'm afraid.

Also typical: on the way home I tried to smooth everything over, this way. I said, "A man rides into town on Friday. And he leaves on Friday. But he only stays two days. How can that be?"

"Worm," Todd growled, "would you just be quiet?"

I need to work on my timing.

TWO

It didn't take me long to figure out what Todd was up to. I mean, come on — here's what he did after we got home from Pizza Hut:

1. Brought the roadmap in from the car and studied it when he thought no one was looking.

2. Asked Mom if she'd finished washing his wool socks.

3. Told Mom it was OK, he'd stay up late and put them in the dryer if she was tired.

4. Drank a cup of coffee before he went to bed.

5. Made interesting noises in his bedroom after he supposedly went to bed. I heard his closet opening, I heard something scrape the floor, I heard all

his dresser drawers opening and shutting. (It's a pretty thin wall between our rooms.)

So I went downstairs and started doing some preparing myself. I may be the Worm, but I'm not stupid.

So when he left the house about two in the morning, with his big frame pack on his back and his hiking staff in his hand and his wool socks on his feet, guess who was waiting on the patio for him. Guess who emerged from the shadows, like a phantom, with his pack on his back.

"WORM!"

I thought Todd was going to have a triple heart attack, right there in the backyard. Talk about having a cow — he was having a mastodon.

"Shhhhh!" I said. "You'll wake up Mom."

"You are NOT coming with me. That's it."

"Why not, Todd? He's my father too!"

"You're eleven years old. You'll slow me up. Forget it."

"Eleven and eleven-twelfths," I said, and then I had a choice. I could say something, the sort of thing I'd never said to Todd before, or I could start to cry. It was then or never.

Two seconds before I started bawling (because it was the only way to keep from bawling), I said, "I'm coming whether you want me to or not."

"Is that right?"

"Yes, it is. If you don't let me, I'll wake up Mom."

It was low. I realize that. But I was desperate.

"You would actually do that?" Todd said, and his voice made it sound like I was mutating into a slug right before his eyes.

"Todd, I want to see him just as bad as you do! You can't tell me to stay here!"

Todd looked up at Mom's bedroom window, and back to me, with his lip curled. Then he spun around and stomped off toward the cut-through place in Mr. Knickerbocker's backyard. I followed.

We walked through the empty dark streets of Colonial Park in complete and total silence, with me hustling to keep up and Todd stomping ahead like he was hoping if he wore me out I'd give up. Actually, part of me was already starting to enjoy it. It was so weird being out on those streets in the middle of the night. The latest I'd ever stayed up before was to watch *Sir Graves Ghastly*, and it ended at twelve o'clock. Colonial Park was like a different place, not the same boring streets with nothing but houses on them (four different styles, see, that get repeated every few houses, for exciting variety). I had a lot of fantasies about living in a place where you could walk to a store without its being a major expedition. Where there were people on the streets doing things. There are some streets in Colonial Park you could use for a firing range and never have to worry about hitting anything.

So there I was, walking past my old elementary

school, and past Ken's house, and past Jefferson Way, which is the busy street in Colonial Park; and everything was so dark and quiet that not even the dogs were awake. I pretended I was in a different dimension. The Twilight Zone! When we crossed Jefferson Way, I really really wanted to drop my pants and display my purple underwear to the world (I got it for my birthday). Just because I could do it, and no one but Todd would ever know. I actually stood there and unzipped, but I was afraid Todd would get so far ahead I'd lose him.

Where Colonial Park ends there are some power lines and open space where kids ride dirt bikes and stuff, and then there's a big woods where we have our tree forts and hideouts. It goes on for miles. By the time we crossed under the power lines I couldn't keep my mouth shut anymore. I said: "Todd, where are we going?"

"We are going to Dad's house."

"This is the woods."

"I know this is the woods, Worm. This is also the way to Dad's house."

I just had this sense — if I kept quiet, he'd tell me. He had something so awesomely amazing in his head, he just couldn't resist.

Didn't even take that long. We'd just gotten started down the trail past the smelly creek when Todd said:

"You can follow Accomack Creek."

"To Dad's house?"

"Yeah. It's beautiful. They'll never find me. They'll figure I tried to hitchhike, or walk down Rolling Road. But all I've got to do is follow the creek, and I'll come out half a mile from Dad's new house, according to my map."

"Splendid."

"I'll sleep during the day. I figure I can spend the first day in our old fort because there's no chance anyone will ever find me there. Then when it gets dark, I just walk and follow the creek. Simple."

"*We*, Todd. *We* walk and follow the creek."

"Are you really serious about coming, Worm?"

I sighed, loud enough, I hoped, for him to hear. "What does it look like to you, Todd?"

"Number one, you're not going to be able to keep up. And when you get tired and want to go home, you can't, because then they'll know where I am. Number two, when I get there, I'm going to want to be doing some serious talking with Dad. That's the whole reason for going. To help him get a grip on things. And number three . . ."

Why is it people always like to have three of everything? Just like there are three pigs, and three branches of the government, and there's a holy trinity, not a holy duo. But Todd couldn't think of a third reason, even though he really wanted to. He kept walking and thinking and finally he said, "Why don't you just camp out at the fort for the next two or three days?"

"I am coming, Todd," I whispered. Then I screamed: "I AM COMING WITH YOU!"

Did he answer? You guess. We tromped along through those quiet woods. The only noise was the cicadas in the trees going chhhrrrrr-CHRRRRRR. The only smells were the creek (which smelled like a sewer even though Todd had told me once it was natural, there was sulfur in the water), and my sweat. It was a pretty cool night, since it had rained, but I was so mad I couldn't stop sweating and my sweat had that nasty sour angry smell it gets when you want to cut your big brother's head off.

Finally we came to the fort. It was actually a big hole in the ground with a plywood roof, but Todd and his friends had done a pretty neat job of building it. They'd all stolen shovels from their tool sheds at home and hiked out there and stashed the tools and come back every afternoon for about three months. When they were done they had it seven feet deep, so you could actually stand up in it, and it had a raised place in the middle so the water would drain off, and they'd brought out old furniture they got at Mrs. Kittle's yard sale, and even a rug. It was always kind of damp in there, but so are a lot of people's basements. And of course they had a stash of *Playboys* and foldouts pinned up on the walls. But the roof was all covered over with brush, so no one ever found it and messed it up. It was like a sacred rule with Todd and his friends that every time you left there, you had to put every branch back over the roof just the way you'd found it.

So if he'd wanted to create a place just to hide out in when he ran away, this would have been it. Also, it was on a hill just above Accomack Creek. Perfect.

Todd picked the sticks and leaves off the roof, one by one, and set them in a pile. He grabbed a corner of the sheet of plywood, and grunted: "Uh," and hollered at me, "Are you going to help or are you just going to stand there?" I hate it when people say stuff like that. I hate it because if I hadn't been off in the ozone, wondering whether a worm might wiggle out of the wall while we were sleeping down there and land on our faces or even in our mouths if we were snoring, I would have helped him without him asking. And it's always like that.

We both dragged the plywood off. It was wedged in pretty tight. Todd climbed down first, and when he had his sleeping bag rolled out he called, "OK, Worm," and I climbed down. We dragged the plywood back over us. But I could tell, even though it was as dark as the inside of your stomach down there, that Todd wasn't lying down, he was sitting up. He was running his fingers through his new Army-style crewcut, too. I swear I could tell even that.

"Suppose we're walking along and we see a cop," Todd said. "What do we do?"

"You mean a policeman?" (I never like to call them cops, because once an officer came to school when I was in fifth grade and he told us that that name came from when they used to wear copper buttons, and they don't anymore, and I decided it was a dumb name therefore and I was never going to use it.)

"Yes, that's what I mean, Worm. What would you do?"

"Run as fast as I could."

"All right. What will you do if it rains for the next three days?"

"I brought a raincoat."

"Suppose we run into a place that's total mud?"

"Go right through it and get muddy and get washed off on the other side."

"You wouldn't try to go around it?"

"No, because then you might get too near to houses and we might get seen."

"OK. Suppose it's getting near daylight, and we're in a place that's not very good for setting up camp. Do you keep going and look for a better camp, or just try to make one there?"

That was a tough one. Finally I said, "It depends. It depends on how bad the place is for camping. I mean if it's right by the edge of an A&P parking lot, forget it, but if there are just some houses nearby, and maybe a hill in between, it would be OK."

"You don't think you might be able to find a good place that might not *be* in the woods, if you kept going? Like maybe under a bridge, or inside an abandoned house or something?"

"Well, that's true. Maybe the best thing would be to stop and scout ahead and check it out."

"Yeah," Todd said. "You could do that."

The thing with Todd was he just always wanted to do things the way *he* wanted to do them. I knew he cared about me. I always knew a major reason I didn't get picked on that much in school was that everyone knew Todd would destroy them if they picked on me and he found out.

We both sat there in the dark for a little while. The air was cool down there. It smelled a little like Play-Doh.

Todd didn't lie down, and finally I said, "Todd?"

"Yeah?" he said.

"Why did the chicken cross the road?"

"To get away from Colonel Sanders."

"Because Ronald McDonald wanted to cut off his feet for Chicken McNuggets."

"Let's go to sleep, Worm."

"Did you figure out the one about Friday yet?"

"Go to sleep, Worm."

Just from the way he said it, I knew it was OK. It was OK I was coming. He wasn't so mad anymore. I had passed some kind of test with at least a C.

Todd lay down on top of his sleeping bag, and so did I. We both took off our clothes down to our underwear and lay there pretending to go to sleep. Yeah, right.

After a while I said, "How long do you think it'll take?"

"Three days, easily. It's about twenty-five miles, best I can figure from the roadmap."

"What'll we go through? I mean, is it really all woods?"

"Well . . . there aren't any towns right on the map or anything. Mostly they don't build right up near creeks."

"We should be OK." That sounded so nice, I wanted to say it again. But I didn't, because I knew it would come out sounding stupid.

Finally Todd said, "What else did you bring, Worm?"

"Besides my sleeping bag and my raincoat?"

"Yes."

"I brought a canteen. And my red underwear, and my green underwear, and my checkered shorts, and my jeans with the paisley patch, and three pairs of socks, and my Cowabunga T-shirt, and my Wolverine T-shirt, and a fork and a spoon and a plate I stole from the kitchen, and a Brillo pad I took from the sink, and my trucker's hat, and some rope, and some fishing line, and the *TV Guide* so we can remember which shows we missed, and my old three-inch kaleidoscope in case we get bored, and my Indian-head penny for good luck, and a book."

"Which book?"

"It's called *How to Survive in the Woods.*"

"We're all set."

"And," I said, "I brought the Secret of Marriage."

"You're kidding."

"It's right here in my pack."

I suppose you're wondering how I could carry the Secret of Marriage in a backpack. Allow me to explain. It was in a blue cardboard box, about as big as two fists, and whenever Mom and Dad had a fight — well, before it got really bad — Dad would take this box down from a shelf in his closet and say, "Dear, remember the Secret of Marriage!" And half the time she'd laugh, or at least smile, and the fight would be over. And Dad would never tell us what was in it, just that it was something from when they first met.

"You think that's going to help him?"

"I just wanted to have it with me."

Todd snorted. Then he rustled down against his bag a little bit, and we were quiet for a minute. I was thinking about going to sleep when Todd said, "What did you bring for food?" — and my heart stopped.

I swear, for a split second it stopped beating. If I hadn't sat up, we might have needed an ambulance.

Then my heart was pounding in my head, and I stood up, and I walked toward the little crack we'd left between the plywood and the dirt, and then I walked back to my sleeping bag and sat down again and said, "I left it at home."

THREE

Todd took a deep breath, but he didn't say anything. After a few seconds I couldn't stand it, so I started talking: "I packed food. It's not like I didn't think about it. But it was so crazy, trying to remember all the stuff I needed and not knowing when you were going to leave and not even knowing if you were leaving that night even though I figured you were, I just went out in the backyard and I thought I put it in my pack, I remember putting it in my pack! I had a couple of cans of Dinty Moore Beef Stew in there, and some Pop-Tarts and some bread and cheese and even a chocolate bar I had stashed away on top of the fridge. It's all there."

"You can't go back."

"No. I can't go back."

"Mom might have already called the police."

"She might have."

"Did you bring any money?"

"I don't have any money."

Todd sighed. Just like a parent. I wondered if he was going to offer to put me on an allowance. Right then, if I could have been sure that Mom was asleep, I would have gone home. And stayed.

"It's not the end of the world, actually," he said. "I've got some food for me and cash I brought along for emergencies. We can stop by the 7-Eleven over in Ravenswood . . . no — when we cross Kay Barn Road, and get enough food for you."

I stood there and looked at him. (I could make out his outline a little.) I knew I ought to say "Thank you," but I didn't want to. Something about the way he'd sighed had made it really hard to tell him thank you. Finally I whispered it.

He said, "You're welcome."

He rolled over. I lay down.

I fell asleep as soon as I shut my eyes.

When I woke up I was in an oven. One ray of light was coming through the crack we'd left in our ceiling. So I could see the sweat on my chest, and my arms, and my legs, and my hands — like I needed to see it. Todd was awake too, staring at the ceiling. He said, "Try to go back to sleep. It's only twelve o'clock."

"I have to pee," I said.

"Just be careful."

As I climbed out the battalions of police surrounding our fort aimed their automatic rifles and screamed: "FREEZE." I ran in a zigzag to dodge the hail of bullets, jumped, rolled across the dirt into Sulfur Creek, and swam underwater to freedom with the shouts of my pursuers ringing in my ears.

Really, I just walked over to a tree and peed on it. I looked around, and saw some birds hopping in the leaves. There was the chrrrr-CHRRRRR of the cicadas. There were big tall trees overhead, and pricker bushes down toward the creek. A squirrel was screaming at me from a branch over my head. My sweat cooled on my face.

I ran back to the fort. It wasn't the same old woods. We were runaways now.

"Can we get arrested for doing this, Todd?" I said when I got back inside. "Can they send us to some juvenile home or something?"

"Are you kidding? The worst they might do is make us go see some counselor at school. Who knows — you might get out of math. Want some food?"

We ate cheese and English muffin sandwiches, and some peanuts and raisins, and tried to go back to sleep.

This time I couldn't. I lay there in the heat, and I

thought about that bag of food that was probably still sitting right there on the kitchen counter, and I knew this was it. Todd would tell everyone this story, and I would be the Worm forever. I could see him at lunch at school, sitting with a bunch of his friends all around him, just like those paintings of Jesus at the Last Supper. First he'd finish the entire story of how he ran away, followed Accomack Creek for twenty-five miles, hiked the entire distance in a day and a half, climbed up on the roof with his old man and said, "Come on Dad, let's get down off this roof and start getting real," and Dad did, and how he's doing a lot better now, and, oh by the way, the only thing that went wrong was — you won't believe this — you know my little brother, Worm? He wanted to tag along, so he comes running along with his little backpack he got for Christmas and he's got all his stuff, even a book on how to live in the woods — right? — but he forgot one thing — and right here Todd would pause a minute, and all his friends would lean forward to listen — and Todd would say —

"The food!" And everyone would crack up. The entire cafeteria would turn toward them, and wonder what they were laughing about, and somebody would ask one of Todd's friends what was so funny, and he'd tell them, and then the kid who asked would tell his friend and he'd tell his friend . . .

Did you know I have one of the strangest belly

buttons any kid was ever born with? You know how some belly buttons are "inny" and some are "outy"? Well, mine is so "outy" it looks like a wart. It could be mistaken for a tumor. When I dress in gym I have to stand with my stomach toward the lockers so nobody can see it and realize what a freak I am.

But the freakiest thing about me is my brain. That's what I lay there thinking in that hot fort. Who else has a brain that can remember the name of Spider-Man's cousin who appeared only in issue #3 of *Web of Spider-Man* but can't remember to bring food on a three-day hiking trip?

I figured I was doing the exact right thing, to run away. Only I shouldn't come back. What if I stayed with Dad? I could start at a new school, and no one would know anything about me.

I stood up, and Todd didn't say anything, so I knew he was asleep. I climbed out of the fort, and I stood and looked at the hot woods, and I felt sad again. Oh sure, I'd see the woods when I came to visit Mom. But it wouldn't be the same.

You have to understand, I'm very lucky to live near such a big forest. Where I live they've been building houses and shopping centers like madmen ever since I can remember, so most kids don't have anything bigger than a little park that they can walk to. Every patch of woods gets torn down for houses and every road gets ripped up and widened every three years, it seems like, and some towns get so crowded with cars they can't even have intersections anymore. They build a bridge over where the traffic light used to be so the cars going one way don't ever have to stop and the cars going the other way can just ride right over them and never have to deal with a red light. And then you've got the Beltway, that just goes around and around and you never see a red light. I think that's the true dream of people who live in Fairfax County. Heaven would be a place where there are no red lights.

But my closest thing to heaven is the Accomack woods, and I'm doubly lucky because I got to go down to them even when I was little. Dad would take us. Accomack Creek is about twenty feet wide and very slow and muddy. No whitewater, no waterfalls. Sometimes it hits a sandbar and the water shoots along a little faster on the one side. It swells up in the spring and knocks down trees along its bank and carries them away and there are always some that get snagged, so there's always a log you can cross on. There's always a log you can lie on and fish from or just dream from. There are lots of carp in the creek and even some catfish. I've caught two catfish out of there. You can catch crayfish too, and one time we tried to boil some and make gumbo but it smelled horrible and we threw it away. Deer are coming back. Dad says you used to see them walking down the streets when Colonial Park was first built, but I never remember seeing any until a year ago. Now I find their tracks alongside the creek every time I go there.

I go there a lot, as you might have guessed, like almost every day after school. You'd be amazed how far away from everything you feel. I mean, it's only a fifteen-minute walk back to the power lines, and Colonial Park, and past Colonial Park is Cedar Run, which is another subdivision, and past that another subdivision and on and on, so believe me, it's not wilderness. But it feels like it because hardly anyone goes there except kids — and not really that many of them. Ken and I hardly see anyone down there. You can hear cars but they sound far away. The sound of the creek is louder.

I found a log across the creek and lay down on it and stared at the water and thought how cool Todd's idea was. I had to totally give him credit — it was like he'd figured out how to trick all the roads and buildings. They thought they ruled, but Todd knew there was a little sliver that would take him right through all those roads and buildings and keep him in the woods the whole time. I completely understood how proud he was of himself this time.

I knew he'd blow up if he found me lazing around

the creek where anyone searching for us could see me, and he'd be right. So I only lay on the log a couple of pretty paranoid minutes. But I ducked my head in the creek to cool off before I went back to the fort. You'd be amazed how cool that water is, even in the summer. You're just about to scream because it's burning cold on your hot skin, but then you wait a second and you go: "AAAAAAAH . . ."

I was cooled off enough to go back into the hothouse and actually fall asleep again.

Todd woke me up this time, telling me it was starting to get dark and we'd better get going. "I'll check it out first," he said. He stuck his head out, real slow, and with that new crewcut he looked so much like GI Joe that I almost laughed. He motioned to me with one hand, just like a guy from a World War II movie, and I pushed my pack out and came up behind it.

We spent about fifteen minutes placing the sticks and the brush back exactly the right way. Todd was afraid they'd find the fort and know we'd been there. We walked down to the creek and set out along the beaten-down trail along the bank.

The moon was so bright it sent shadows stretching across our path. The creek was just a dark pit on our left, but you could hear it gurgling and lapping and running where it hit sandbars. I could almost have followed that trail blindfolded, I'd walked it so many times — past the old metal dam that the creek just ran right over the top of, and the boggy spot that turned into a big pond in the spring when the creek ran high, and the S-bend where logs and sticks always jammed up and junk got stuck against them and sometimes you could find logs big enough to float on, and then the flat quiet stretch where the creek seemed more like a canal and it went past a hill with big white rocks. When it flowed into Lake Accomack we had to follow along the shore until we came up to the old railroad bed. It's a walking trail because the trains haven't run on it for eighty years, and Todd and I walked side by side in the dark. The trail stretched straight ahead for a quarter of a mile before it bent, and in the moonlight you could see that whole distance. Where the darkness started up again I could picture all the new bends and boggy places and roads and hills and faces we might see waiting ahead.

Then the trail cut away from the old railroad bed and went through the woods along the dam. This was an official Fairfax County Park Authority trail, and I think we were both wondering if we should stay on the trail or try to cut through the woods so we wouldn't be seen. How weird to be worrying about being seen at Lake Accomack.

We passed an old lady with a poodle, and a kid on a bike. Neither of them turned out to be undercover.

We came to the Lake Accomack Dam. I stood on the lookout platform on one side of the dam, and I could see the picnic area, where Dad had been feeding those ducks. I said, "Did you leave a note for Mom?"

"Yeah. Come on, we don't want to hang around here."

"What did it say?" I asked him as we jogged down the trail to the base of the dam, with our packs bouncing on our backs.

"What was I going to tell her? 'I'm following the creek to Dad's house'? I think I told her not to worry about me."

"That was nice."

"Poor her! We wouldn't even be doing this if she hadn't kicked Dad out."

Todd had never said that before. Even though I knew he thought it. All of a sudden I felt nervous, I guess because I knew I had to say something back, and it was like I was being called on in class when I didn't know the answer. Finally I said:

"I think it's hard on her, too."

"She didn't have to kick him out, did she? Who made her kick him out?"

What I remembered was, they agreed to separate. And then he left. And she stayed. I always had the feeling it was more her idea than his.

"You know what?" I said. "I bet she's never spent

a night alone in that house." (Even when Dad and Todd and I went camping, she'd invite her sister from North Carolina up.)

"She'll be OK, Worm."

"Are you mad at her for not letting us visit Dad?"

"I'm NOT MAD at her, Worm!"

"Got it."

We were both quiet for a while. Where the trail went under a railroad bridge, there were a bunch of boulders and big rocks and we had to hop and step real careful. But when we got a little past the bridge, Todd said, "I still love her, Worm." "I know," I said, and I felt embarrassed. I felt like Todd had been reading my mind. I was thinking that the reason he's so mad at her is he always looked up to her so much. He used to braid her hair for her, just last year! How many thirteen-year-old boys do you know who'd braid their mother's hair? He was always the one who organized her birthday party and picked out most of her presents, and one year he even called all her relatives in North Carolina and had a surprise party for her, even though it was just her forty-first birthday. That made it a real surprise. I think he was only eleven when he did that. I couldn't call up that many adults and get them to come to my house in a million years.

But when you're that close to someone, it's even harder when they let you down.

Good thing we were starting on the unknown part of our trip just then, because it gave us both something else to think about. I mean, now we were on the part of the creek that neither of us had ever walked on before. I kept glancing around in the dark to see if there would be different rocks, or new kinds of trees, or if there would be black squirrels or red squirrels there. Dumb, of course, because we knew we were going to come to Kay Barn Road, which we'd ridden over a million times before. But it felt as though we were entering a foreign land.

One thing missing was a trail along the creek. Or if there was one, we weren't finding it. We were crashing through honeysuckle bushes for a while, getting our hands and faces all sticky and our noses all full of that sweet-sweet smell. Then there was a little stretch where the bank of the creek was all washed out and there were prickers coming right up to the edge, so we had to tiptoe along a log and a real narrow sandbar and hope we didn't fall into the water. The creek still smelled the same, kind of musty and fishy, and if the trees were different, I couldn't tell. They were just big shapes in the dark. The straps of my pack were digging into my shoulders and I could already tell the exact spot where my hiking boots were going to give me a blister. My hiking boots pick a different blister spot every time I use them. I asked Todd, "Knock, knock," and he actually answered me, "Who's there?"

"Ach!"

"Ach-who?"

"Gesundheit!"

He even laughed a little bit, I think. We were splashing across a feeder creek at that point, so it was a little hard to hear.

I think we were both surprised when we came to Kay Barn Road. It wasn't supposed to show up so quick. And it was funny to climb up away from the creek and the darkness and the crickets and cicadas chirping and find yourself back on Kay Barn Road, under a streetlight, trying to remember which way the 7-Eleven was.

I said, "What do you think Mom did when she figured out we were gone?"

"Called the police, of course."

"I wonder what the police do. I mean, do they get out the bloodhounds and the helicopters, or do they just say they'll keep an eye out for us?"

"Let's play it safe," Todd said. "Let's figure bloodhounds."

We stashed our packs under the bridge so as not to look suspicious. I think it was already about ten o'clock. Nights are so short in June.

We crossed the road and walked into the 7-

Eleven just like normal people. Todd picked out the food, and I didn't say anything because it was his money. Unfortunately, he got a couple of cans of split pea soup, which remind me a little of that mucus you get in the back of your throat if you've had a cold for a long time, the kind that you can't ever swallow down so it's always there? And he got some of the macaroni and cheese you make out of a box, which to me tastes like tree bark. And I know, because one time Ken and I tried to eat some tree bark. And then he got some Ramen noodles, which just look too much like worms for me. (Don't ask how I ate the real worm when I was a little kid. Since then I've become pretty picky about food, actually.) But he did get some Cap'n Crunch cereal, which is excellent for camping because no matter how many times you stuff a bag of it into a pack and take it out again, it never gets ground up into a million pieces, the way cornflakes do.

When we brought all the stuff up to the counter, I picked up a couple of Hershey bars and set them down and smiled my nicest smile at Todd. He just shrugged, and didn't put them back, so I knew he wasn't that mad at me anymore.

We got all the stuff in a shopping bag and Todd paid. The woman behind the counter told us to have a nice day (even though it was dark and the day was practically over — I hate it when they do that). We headed for the door and there, in the 7-Eleven doorway, with his fists on his hips, stood Mr. Harris.

Todd's football and track coach. My gym teacher. We both knew, from the way he stared at us, that he knew we'd run away. Of course, I thought as I stood there with no saliva in my mouth, Mom called the school and everyone there knows.

"How about we put an end to this little adventure?" he said.

Todd kicked me in the ankle and started walking toward the opposite set of doors from where Mr. Harris was standing. (7-Elevens always have long glass front walls and two sets of double doors.)

"Uh, gentlemen —" (He always called kids gentlemen, or ladies.) "Gentlemen, may I have the honor of an answer?"

Todd gave him his answer all right. He dropped the grocery bag and ran. I was right behind him. Mr. Harris was quick, though. There probably wasn't another teacher in the school who could have run out the doors on his side and right down the little sidewalk to our doors as fast as he did. But all he got for his trouble was a door smack in his face, as we came charging out of there. I actually looked at him as we ran, because I was so scared, and the look on his face as he was staggering backward was the kind of look our cat got one time when we showed it a mirror and it kept trying to go around behind the mirror to find this new cat and it couldn't.

He was behind us as we ran across the parking lot. I ran so hard, I was out of breath before I got halfway across. How was I going to run faster than Mr. Harris? He coached track in the spring! I had a good head start, because it took him a minute after the door hit his face to get going. But I could hear his sneakers slapping pavement behind us, getting closer. And Todd was getting ahead of me.

I almost stopped at the edge of Kay Barn Road because I was afraid we'd get hit by cars. But I couldn't. I couldn't let myself get nailed by Mr. Harris. We burst across Kay Barn Road right in front of a pack of cars bearing right down on us. I ran like a mush-dog with a whip on it. I ran so hard I had no brain anymore, just some muscles and some pure fear, and all I could do was go right over the median strip and across the four lanes on the other side, just ahead of another pack of cars speeding at us at sixty miles an hour. But we made it to the other side. We never looked back. We plunged into a patch of woods on the other side, and all of a sudden we were tripping and stumbling over roots and branches and getting torn at by prickers. Out of the woods, look out, here we come, but now there was a long string of baseball fields and basketball courts in front of us. Big recreation area.

Todd ran straight for a baseball game. I hissed —

not enough breath to yell — "Todd! Where are you going?"

He yelled back, "Come ON!" and I had no choice.

We ran right across the pitcher's mound. In the middle of a game. It was fun, and scary and weird at the same time. People didn't even have a chance to yell at us. We were like ghosts. It was an adult softball game, and we were floating right through it. The people were so surprised, they mostly just stared. We ran across a basketball court with three guys fast-breaking right at us. One guy fell down when he saw us, and I jumped right over him and we kept going, just ghosts, leaping over a fence with one hand on the crossbar and sprinting across the outfield of another grown-up softball game where the right fielder was circling around under a ball that someone had actually hit to him out there.

Across a little patch of tall grass, into another subdivision (I'd never been in this one, even though it couldn't have been more than four miles from my house), down some streets. I was really more jogging by then. I was completely whipped. And now that we didn't have an audience, and we didn't have Mr. Harris behind us, I really felt it.

Todd just kept going. He never even looked back. We ran down some streets, but all I remember is my tongue feeling like it was three sizes too big in my mouth, and my chest about to split open. My legs felt like they were stuck in quicksand, but I kept sticking them into the quicksand and pulling them back out again.

We got back to the creek. I don't know how Todd knew the way. He must have just guessed. I thought, YES! We can stop running. He didn't. There was a paved bike path along that stretch of the creek and Todd ran down it. I said, "Stop. Please."

He heard me and turned around. "We can't," he said. "They'll look for us here."

"OK," I said. He was right. I wasn't about to get caught after all that. I tried closing my eyes and running, thinking maybe it'd be easier if I couldn't see myself.

Finally, we made it back to where we'd stashed the packs. No time to lose here, either. We put our packs on and started marching right back down that bike path, the way we'd just come. At least we weren't running now. But we were walking pretty darn fast. We couldn't help it — we both felt like police might jump out of the bushes any second.

I said, "Can I ask you why you wanted to run straight across a ballfield? When you know the police will be looking for us here?"

"They'll ask all those people who saw us. And those people will tell them we ran into that subdivision."

"Oh."

"So they'll think we're going that way, toward Backlick Road, and not following the creek."

"Right."

It was very smart; what could I say? For him to be thinking about all that at the same time he was trying to run away from Mr. Harris — I was impressed.

At one point I was seriously going to ask Todd to stop so I could check if there was a boulder in my pack. Good thing I didn't. But I don't remember anything about that stretch of the creek. I know the bike path ended pretty soon, and we were on some kind of dirt road for a little way, and then just a little trail. I kept telling myself we'd quit and catch our breath when we got to that big black patch of trees up ahead, and then I told myself we'd quit when we got to that place up ahead where it looked like the trail curved, and then I told myself we'd quit after ten more steps, then five more steps, and that way I kept going.

Of course neither of us noticed how heavy the air was getting. It was getting that damp, heavy feeling, and a tiny little wind was picking up, and if we'd been paying any attention we would have known what that meant.

This rain just started, flat-out pouring. Most rainstorms give you a little warning, like a few drops just to let you know they're coming. We were drenched in about two minutes. We stopped and got our raincoats on, but we were already soaked by then. It probably would have made more sense just to strip naked. And of course I'd strapped my sleeping bag onto the bottom of the pack so now I had to try to stuff it in the top to keep it dry, but I could barely tie the top flap back down when I was done stuffing, and parts of it bulged out, and I had to walk along being wet and worrying about my bag getting wetter behind me and what it would be like to sleep in a wet sleeping bag that night. Plus, my tongue was sore, and I couldn't remember how it got sore, if I bit it or what, and I hate having a sore tongue because it makes you think about your tongue. You keep thinking about how it sits there in your mouth, all fat and wet and pale, and how it will always be there until the day you die. But I guess at least it gave me something to think about besides the rain, and the way the wetness was creeping up my boots because every step made a splash and the water flew up as high as my socks and then trickled down inside my socks and started seeping down toward my toes. It was dark, like I had my eyes shut. But I could hear the thunder rumbling, to make me a little more nervous. I know, eleven years old, right? But it sounded like the sky was going to break.

The heavy rain quit after not too long, but the

storm hung around and kept sprinkling and dumping little showers on us and the trees were dripping. We didn't have much of a trail to follow, and brushing against the bushes alongside the creek was like going through a carwash. And then we came to the swamp.

FOUR

There was one problem with Todd's plans. All he had was a roadmap to plan with. But why do they call them roadmaps? Because they only show roads. Maybe here and there a mountain, with a little cross to mark it. No swamps.

The ground started sucking at our boots. The air began to smell like all the dirt under us had turned rotten. There weren't so many bushes there, just trees spaced apart, looking lonely. And it seemed even darker than it had five minutes before. I know it couldn't have been, but it seemed like we'd walked into a cave so big we hadn't even noticed where the walls were yet. If I'd bumped into a stalagmite I wouldn't have been surprised. Just then I sank into the muck. Into the yuck. Right up to my thigh.

"Todd," I said. I thought I sounded real calm, but he came hustling over. He pulled me out, suuuck-plup. I sank in again. I don't know how he got me out, because he was sinking, too. It was like we'd walked into a pond of mud. But he held my hand, and we sucked and plupped away from the creek.

What was sort of neat was, neither of us said, "Let's go this way." You know how sometimes you can look at someone's eyes, and automatically know what they're thinking? It was like that, except we couldn't see each others' faces. Of course, I don't know what else we were going to do — walk into the creek? It might have been better than the swamp.

But that swamp just kept going. So we kept dragging through the mud. After a little while we didn't care how putrid our legs got. And after a little while more, we didn't care how putrid our arms got. And after a little while more, we might as well have stuck our heads into it and wiggled around. We'd climb out onto little humps of grass, and then take a step and the ground would just sink under us. Sluuuurp.

It got a little better, the farther we walked. It got to where the grass humps were closer together so you could sort of hop from one to the other. And then we came to a chainlink fence.

It was the seven-foot-high kind, like they use to fence off reservoirs. Todd took off his pack and tried to throw it over, but the pack caught at the top; he caught the pack as it fell back, so it knocked him down in the mud. He jumped up and and climbed halfway up the fence with one hand while still holding the pack with the other hand. Then he reared back and threw it as hard as he could and his pack went flying and bounced off a tree on the other side. My pack was a little harder to get over because the sleeping bag kind of drooped off the top. It caught on the top of the fence when I climbed partway up and tried to hand it over to Todd, who was standing with his feet in the fence on the other side, reaching up. He got hold of my pack but the sleeping bag caught on the spiky wire on the top of the fence, and for a second he was kind of stuck with the sleeping bag caught there while he tried to climb down backwards, but then something ripped and he fell back on his side while my sleeping bag made a splatting sound on my side. I tried to catch it. It was pretty easy to throw over the fence, though, by itself. Todd made a noise in his throat when he caught it.

I got over the fence OK, once all my stuff was on the other side. With my pack on my back and my slimy sleeping bag in my arms and Todd saying something nasty under his breath we kept walking, right into someone's backyard.

Turns out they'd built a subdivision right up to the edge of the swamp. We walked right past someone's kitchen window. Their lights were all out, but then a dog started barking, right next to us it sounded like, and we took off running. We ran even after we couldn't hear the dog anymore, Todd saying words I'd never heard him say before, and me hustling to keep up. Good thing it was the middle of the night. I guess we might have attracted some attention otherwise.

I was actually the one who finally talked. I said, "Stop." And Todd actually stopped. I said, "Todd?" and he said, "Yes, Worm." I said, "What did one raisin say to the other?" "Worm," he said, "we've got to find a place." "Nothing," I said, "raisins don't talk." "We've got to find a place to stop," Todd said, and I told him, "You're right."

There were still quite a few hours of dark left, but forget it. We were walking down the street past all these houses with no trees in the backyards. No trees anywhere, and it gave me the creeps. There was no place to run to. The street went down a long hill and then a creek passed under it — just a little creek but it had woods all along its edges. We scrambled down a culvert and followed the creek downstream until there was a little more woods, enough to feel safe, and that's where we set up Todd's tent, which for some reason hadn't come off when his pack hit that tree. We unrolled the fly for the tent, and the tent, and got all the stakes out, and couldn't find some of the stakes, and Todd's flashlight was waving around like he was one of those guys who guides airplanes in. We finally left the middle part of the tent without any stakes and threw our wet sleeping bags in there and crawled in, and lay there with our filthy clothes in smelly little piles beside us.

At least it wasn't cold.

It took us about ten minutes to find Todd's can opener in the bottom of his pack. Stuff was all over the floor of the tent, getting muddy, and by the time we got some beef stew cooked up on his backpacking stove, I think the beef stew was muddy too. We split it. I was still starving when it was done. Did I complain?

We tried to sleep, but I was wide awake. I knew Todd was, too. After a while I asked him:

"What kind of food have you got left?"

"Enough," he said right away, so I knew he'd been lying there thinking about it too. "We'll just be on short rations till we get to Dad's."

Short rations? We were playing Army.

But all of a sudden I felt scared. I thought . . . What if Todd actually is treating this like a game? I mean, I knew he wasn't, but what if he was *partly* acting like it was a game? What if he was treating it *too much* like playing Army? In other words, what if he didn't really completely know what he was doing?

Even with the swamp-stink in that tent, I could smell the smell of Todd in there. I can't exactly describe it for you, except to say it reminded me a little of when you come home from summer vacation and open up your dresser drawer, and that smell would make you feel safe. Whenever I'd be in trouble at school, or someone would be teasing me really hard, or Mom or Dad were mad at me, I'd go into Todd's room and feel better. Even if he wasn't there. Just from the smell.

So it scared the you-know-what out of me to think — I mean, seriously consider the possibility — that Todd was making mistakes. Maybe big-time. Because right then it seemed like about a thousand miles to Dad's house.

I think I came pretty close, for a few minutes there. I was just about to walk out of that tent, walk to the nearest house and ask if I could use the phone. I was that close to weaselhood. In fact, I did lie and tell Todd I had to pee. I stood next to the tent and looked at the back of a house I could see through the trees because they had a floodlight on above their basement doorway. I thought about how quick Mom would get there if I called, and how she'd probably be so glad to see us she wouldn't even get mad, just take us home and make us hot chocolate. I'm not kidding, more than anything it was the hot chocolate that almost made me do it. Try sleeping in a wet bag with your breakfast and your next couple of days' meals sort of questionable, and you'll know why.

But I didn't go, and the reason was I managed to think about what I would do after that hot chocolate. What I would do when I had to face my friends and tell them what had happened. What I'd say to Todd, how I would manage to live in the same house with him if I stabbed him in the back like that. And I thought about Dad.

I got back in the wretched tent and lay there for a moment. Then Todd said, "We can't call Mom," and I jumped up.

"Who said anything about calling Mom?"

"I mean we ought to call her just to tell her we're OK. I mean, it's not like they're going to trace a phone call on us."

"She's not going to sleep tonight."

"But if I call her, I might tell her. Where we are, I mean."

"You would? Why?"

"What if I just say it? What if she goes, 'Todd, oh my God, where are you?' with that voice of hers and I just spit it out? 'We're following Accomack Creek, Ma!' I might actually do that, Worm. I really might."

I lay back down. Slowly. My skin went *Oooooo* when it knew it had to feel that nasty cold tent floor. I'll never know. I'll never know if Todd was lying in his sleeping bag just then, thinking, "I want to go home but I can't betray Worm." I'll never know if that's why he brought up Mom right then. I'll never know because I never will ask him. But if he'd suddenly crawled out of the tent just then and said, "Worm, why don't we just pack it up?" . . . in a heartbeat.

Why hadn't I brought a sleeping pad? I knew I had to say something to Todd but the only thing I could think of was, "Remember the time we put the living room out in the front yard for April Fool's Day?"

"That was just a couple of years ago," Todd said.

"Seems like longer."

"I never do stupid things anymore."

"You've got to get straight A's and get into UVA and run track and be a lawyer, right?"

"It'd be good for me," Todd said. "I ought to put the living room out on the lawn again and sit out there and watch TV all night."

"I think it was actually Bannon who came up with the idea," I said. "But you got it organized."

"I think it was actually your idea to get the extension cords."

Yes, it was my idea — I sure was glad he remembered that.

I said, "Remember the look on Mom's face when she came home?"

"Yes."

"The greatest thing was, she didn't look like even

for one second she ever thought about being mad. It was like first she wondered what the heck was going on, then she remembered it was April Fool's, and then she laughed."

Todd said, "I remember the way she laughed."

I lay there and listened to him remember for a minute. Then I rolled over. I got the Secret of Marriage out of my bag and set it on top of my boots, thinking somehow it would dry out that way. I was really worried the bottom of the box would fall out from being wet. I wanted to put on some dry clothes, but I was afraid the sleeping bag would get them wet. Finally I kicked the bag off and put some dry clothes on and lay down with no bag. But I'd forgotten Todd was still lying there thinking. All of a sudden he said:

"You've got to figure out a way to get some more food, Worm. I can't keep doing everything."

"OK." I said. What else could I say? Did I have the slightest idea how I was going to find food?

How I ever fell asleep I don't know. I guess my body was so beat it finally forced my mind to shut up.

FIVE

I don't think I slept long. When I woke up the sun was up. I climbed out of the tent, looked around, and tried to figure how high in the sky it was, but too many trees were in the way. Beech trees, some with initials carved in them.

I looked around a little more and saw a fence, about as far from us as a teacher's desk is from the kid in the back corner, and behind that fence a swing set and behind that swing set a house. I sure hoped the people who lived there weren't taking the day off. Right next to that house, of course, was another house and right next to that was another, and the big backs of all the houses with their decks and their patios and their screened-in porches were all looking at us like, "What do you think this is, Yosemite?"

I woke up Todd and told him maybe we'd better get going.

Putting the muddy stakes into their little bag, rolling up the wet tent with the ground squishing under our feet, I felt like a towel that's just been used to dry off someone's most intimate parts and then thrown into a corner of a locker room for other people to step on. You know how your toes get if they stay wet too long? All pale and flaky? I felt like my face must look like that.

But we got everything together and started walking again. Right away we found where our little creek ran into Accomack Creek — and there was no swamp! Todd and I just kind of looked at each other when we reached the bank of Accomack Creek, and it was just nice and firm, like: Do we get on our knees and kiss the sand? But we didn't. We just kept on walking.

The major problem was that it was pure broad daylight, and we weren't supposed to be out in daylight. But there was no place to set up the tent again and hide for the day. This was another thing that Todd's map didn't show — how much woods were there alongside the creek? In this spot, the creek cut between little hills on either side, and right on top of the hills were the fences with their leaf piles and tool sheds right up against them.

We walked through the ravine, both of us scrunched down a little. Once a car engine started up, and we both jumped. The trees were still dripping a little, but it was real warm. A warm breeze was blowing right up along the creek. You could smell where someone had just cut the lawn nearby.

Todd said, "We're going to have just keep going till we find a place," and right then I spotted something.

A tree house. Just like the one we'd built up along our stretch of the creek. Not really a house, just a platform set where the base of a tree grew out into three big branches. It was about ten feet off the ground. I stopped Todd and said, "We can hide up there."

"There?"

"We'll take the fly from the tent and wrap it around those big branches and that tree fort platform will be like the floor. Todd. It's perfect."

"I think we'd better keep going."

"You just don't want to admit I'm right."

"People will see it. There are houses right up there."

"They're all at work. Anyway, they won't see us because we'll be behind the fly. And I guarantee, they won't notice that the fly wasn't up there yesterday. Unless they're kids they won't notice, and we don't have to worry about kids."

He didn't say anything, so I knew I had him.

"Would you rather keep walking? You think people won't see us then?"

"OK!" he said, "All right! All right . . ."

The tent fly didn't want to stay wrapped around those trees, but we got some rocks and pinned down the corners of it pretty tight. The top sort of sagged, so it wasn't quite the way I pictured it, but if we scrunched down we were definitely out of sight. Best of all, the sun shone. The beautiful shining warm sun came out for us, and that platform was wide enough so we could spread our stuff out and let it dry. First I set out my Wolverine T-shirt, because I was really worried about the ink maybe smearing (I still collect comics, Marvel only), and then my checkered shorts, because they had power, they always made me feel at least one year older, then my Cowabunga T-shirt, which was getting a little out of date, then my jeans with the paisley patch because I had a feeling I wasn't going to wear them unless the weather cooled down, then my red underwear, then my green underwear, which left me with nothing to wear. I put the Secret of Marriage upside down in a spot where the sun shone especially hot, and we lay there butt-naked with that sun soaking into our skin and began to feel like human beings again. I don't remember another time when my entire body felt so good, from any fingernails right down to my small intestine. It was like being hugged by the sun. Todd smelled like a swamp next to me, but I didn't care because I smelled like a swamp, too. After a while I rolled over on my back, and fell asleep in three seconds.

When I woke up the sun was right overhead and I was sweating hard. Todd was sleeping. I took a granola bar from his pack and ate it. It just made me hungrier, so I took another one and ate it. I didn't feel sleepy but I didn't feel like doing anything much. I lay there for a while thinking about the stuff I always think about (if I'm not worrying): my bellybutton, and whether surgery could correct it; toejam, which is the stuff that collects under your toenails and which I don't think you ever get cleaned out completely even if you clip your toenails and use an old toothbrush to scrub with, which means that even Natalie Berdan (the most beautiful girl in school) has some toejam under her toenails if you really looked; and what it would be like to be a paraplegic. But after a while I began to think about what Todd had said last night, about my finding food.

For me, one way of dealing with a problem is to find a book about it. I never exactly find the answer, but at least reading gets my mind off my worries. So I found my copy of *How to Survive in the Woods*, which was one of the few things that hadn't gotten seriously wet, and started to read. The first section I turned to was the one on trapping food.

We were still about two nights' walk from Dad's

place. We had a regular-sized can of chili, four granola bars (since I'd just eaten two — yes, I was really feeling guilty), one hard roll and some cheese, and half a chocolate bar. In other words, we had one day's food for two people. So it wasn't like we were going to starve to death. Still, it was looking like a pretty hungry walk, and I knew Todd hadn't completely stopped being mad at me. *I* hadn't stopped being mad at me. So as I sat there reading about snaring squirrels and rabbits, it sounded impossible, but it also sounded pretty interesting. I found that piece of rope I'd stuck in my pack. It was wet.

My checkered shorts were a little stiff from drying out, but I put them on. I climbed down on the little scraps of two-by-four nailed into the tree for steps, and looked around.

I wished I had my shirt on. Those backyards at the top of the hill were seeing how skinny I am. I swung that rope around my head, like I was daring someone to notice me, and I started looking around for signs.

The book said to find a rabbit trail or a squirrel trail, and I figured a squirrel trail was the best bet. I knew if those woods were anything like the woods near my house, they'd by infested with squirrels. Even our backyard at home was crawling with squirrels, because the developer who built Colonial Park left lots of trees in all the yards. My Mom had tried a hundred different strategies for keeping them out of the bird feeder. One time she hung the bird feeder from the middle of the clothesline, and they walked upside down on the clothesline to get to it. "Bushy-tailed tree rats," my father called them.

Their nests were easy to spot. I found one way up high in an oak tree, and looked around the base of the tree. But there wasn't much sign. No acorn caps. I lay down on my belly and stared at the ground right around the base of the tree and tried to see if I could spot any squirrel tracks. Now I wasn't *real* sure I could see squirrel tracks even if they were there, but I finally decided I had a dud tree. I *had* to be real sure before I set my snare. The ground under the tree was all sticky and pasty and it seemed to me a squirrel might actually have left a mark there if he had been by.

I wandered away from the tree fort, checking out the bases of trees. At each one, I'd flop down on my belly just the way the book said, to see if I could spot tracks or at least a "shining." A shining was supposed to be a place where grass or leaves had been pushed down slightly by an animal passing through, so that the sunlight struck it differently. The book said sometimes you could see a little path of light. I didn't see any path of light, but under one tree I did find what I was sure were tracks. I was so excited, I hopped. I remembered squirrel tracks from the snow — the two little paws right near the long ones — and I put my cheek down right next to this slick drying-out mud under one tree, and touched them very gently, because the book said sometimes you could feel the shape of tracks, and I knew this was my tree.

So I propped a stick up against it, the way the book said, the idea being that if you give a squirrel an easy path off a tree, that's the way he'll go. There was a branch right above where the tip of my stick touched the trunk of the tree, and I tied one end of my rope to that. Then I took the end that was hanging down and tied a slipknot in that end, just the way the book said . . . well, maybe not *exactly* the way the book said. The book had this idea that anyone who read it would be an experienced outdoors type who always wore suspenders and waterproof boots and already knew how to tie a slipknot. I had learned in Boy Scouts, but I'd quit Boy Scouts about three years before because the meetings were on the same nights *The Simpsons* was on. So I spent about three hours, it seemed like, trying to remember how to tie a stupid slipknot and thinking how last year I'd officially decided I hated *The Simpsons* because my jokes were funnier.

I finally got the knot. I had the end of the rope tied to a branch, and the noose set on the tip of the stick, but it didn't look right. I couldn't imagine any self-respecting squirrel actually coming down a tree and getting trapped in that thing. I could see myself coming back to that tree and all the squirrels would be sitting up in the branches saying, "Ha ha ha, what book were you reading, kid? *How to Survive in the Woods?* You really believe that stuff?" I told myself I'd sneak back over there before we left and take the rope down before Todd saw it, so I wouldn't have to explain.

I walked back with my head down, noticing things. That's the great thing about tracking and trying to trap animals, as I learned later on. If you start noticing a few things, you start noticing everything. I noticed that some sticks that were caught in a logjam on the creek had teeth marks on them from beavers' gnawing. I noticed some people tracks in a sandy place and I squatted down and took a really good look at them and decided they were pretty new. The edges of the tracks were still there, where with older tracks the edges would have crumbled some. I noticed some grass that had been clipped off, so after I checked in my book I figured it was probably deer that had eaten it because deer snip off leaves and branches but most other animals — dogs, for instance — chew on them and the parts that are left in the ground are sort of mashed-up looking. And I noticed I was going to get a sunburn from sitting in that tree fort naked with no lotion on.

I noticed how some high-up clouds were coming across the sky. I noticed how a little tiny wind made the leaves on the trees shake. I noticed how the sun hit some ripples in the creek and made them look like light beating.

But I didn't notice the two kids who were standing under the tree fort talking to Todd. Not until I'd almost walked up on them.

SIX

I think they were only a couple of years older than Todd. One of them had on that kind of uniform you wear if you want everyone to think you're BAD. You know, a jean jacket with no sleeves, black boots, and a Harley-Davidson T-shirt, with maybe an earring in your nose if you really want to take chances. So you look just like all the other kids who want to be BAD. The other one, for some reason I never figured out, was wearing jeans, a flannel shirt (with sleeves rolled up) and a wool cap on his head. He was staring at Todd and smiling like he had some bad news he was really going to get a kick out of sharing. He had real skinny arms. When I walked up he was telling Todd this was his tree fort. Todd was pulling his clothes back on. He didn't say a word until he had all his clothes on.

"We built it," Wool Cap said.

"We borrowed it," Todd said. "OK?"

"We want it back."

"Come on, Worm. I guess we're moving on."

"What are you guys," said Harley-Davidson, "on a hiking trip?"

"I guess you could say that."

"Well, we're the inspectors," said Wool Cap. "We reserve the right to inspect all baggage that passes through our fort."

"I don't think so," said Todd. "Look, my brother and I just want to get going. I don't think you want any grief, do you?"

God, I loved him right then. He knew I wasn't worth a thing in any fight; he knew it'd be two-on-one. But he didn't think twice. He just wasn't about to back down to anyone. Why should he? He'd never lost a fight in his life. He was three inches taller than anyone else in the ninth grade, and he looked like a surfer from one of those dumb old beach movies. There we were, runaways in some strange woods without enough food and two older kids looking for grief with us, and I couldn't have felt safer.

Until Wool Cap took out a gun.

I couldn't believe I hadn't noticed it before. He had it stuck in the back of his pants, where Todd couldn't see it, but I could have.

Todd's mouth dropped open, and it seemed like a long time before he shut it again. While I was waiting for my big brother to shut his mouth — that's when all my safe feeling flew away.

Todd said, "Just let us go. We don't want any problems."

"Nor I with you," said Wool Cap. "We just want to inspect your things."

"Hey," said Harley-Davidson, "Jay —"

Wool Cap just poked a skinny elbow in Harley's chest, and Harley shut up.

"Bring the stuff down here," said Wool Cap. Now Todd had to throw the stuff into the packs, climb down out of the tree fort, set the packs down in front of Wool Cap, and empty them out, thing by thing.

Wool Cap waved the gun at me and made me stand over near Todd. I had a good line — "Where'd you get that move from, *Man from U.N.C.L.E.* reruns?" Did I say it?

Todd arranged all our stuff along the roots of the tree, like it was going to be in a picture in some catalogue. There was all his practical stuff: compass, cookset, stove, canteen, extra socks, and all my mostly stupid stuff, including the one thing I'd kill for: the Secret of Marriage. I noticed one other thing that I didn't even know I'd brought. They must have been in the pack left over from some other trip. Fishhooks.

"We confiscate stuff too," said Wool Cap Robber. "It's like a rental fee."

He picked up the canteen and I could just about smell the rage coming off Todd. If he ever met that kid someplace else, with no gun around . . .

Didn't help now. The slime-speck picked up our extra clothes, still with that gun pointed at Todd. He picked up our one can of chili. He said, "I wish I had a bag. Henry, why don't you give me a hand?"

"Hey," Henry said, looking at my book, which I was trying to stuff up my shirt, "are you the guys who ran away?"

"How do you know about it?"

Henry actually smiled at Todd. "We talk to the local cops a lot," he said. "They sort of check in with us every night. Just because we hang around in the park."

"Very close connection," said the seropurulent thief.

"They told us some kids had run away and might be coming through here and we should keep an eye out for them," said Henry.

"But you won't tell the cops," said Todd.

Henry raised his arms with both hands kind of hanging off his wrists, and shrugged and said, "We're not exactly real good friends with the cops."

"What did you run away for?" said the weasel as he put Todd's compass in his pocket.

"I'm going to find you," Todd said. "I'm going to find you if it takes the rest of my life."

"I'm moving to Hawaii next week. After I sell all your stuff!" He whooped and whack-whacked hands with Henry. But Henry didn't seem that into it. I said to him, "We went to buy extra food and we ran into my gym teacher. Can you believe that? He tried to chase us."

"No kidding," said the bacteria as he hung the canteen over his shoulder. "How did you get away?"

"We ran like crazy. Then we doubled back, and found our stuff, and got stuck in a swamp."

"You walked through the Badlands?" said Henry. "Last time I went into the Badlands I was about nine years old and I thought I was going to die. I thought I was going to get eaten by the quicksand."

"We almost did die," I said, but no one was listening.

Roadkill picked up the can of chili, and Todd howled, "Just leave us our frigging FOOD!"

They both looked at him. "Jay," said Henry. "Let's leave them their food."

"Why should we? He just told us he owes an entire day's rent on our tree fort."

"Leave us our food," Todd said.

"Do it," Henry said. "We can hardly carry all this stuff anyway."

"I'll leave it," said the monster, "if you get down on your knees and say 'pretty please.'"

There's this Superman movie I used to love when I was a kid, where the evil aliens have taken over Earth and demand that the President kneel before them. They're in the White House and somebody comes out of this crowd of guys in suits and kneels. But the evil aliens say that's not the President, nobody with power would kneel that quickly.

This time, I was that guy. I knew Todd would rather get shot than kneel before that gun. So I did, and I said, "Pretty please."

"All right," said the Gun, "'pretty please with maraschino cherries on top.'"

"Pretty please with maraschino cherries on top."

"Very nice." He threw the can of chili in the dirt at Todd's feet. I guess he didn't like chili. Because he took all the rest of the food. He took Todd's backpack, and put all the stuff he'd stolen into it. He told Henry to climb up in the tree and get the sleeping bags. Henry made a face at him, but he did it. He climbed up in the tree, took our sleeping bags, and came back down with them. Then the creature said, "I see something laying right over there next to the tree. Something he kicked when he saw us coming."

Todd looked like he was dying a million times at once. Henry walked around to the far side of the tree, and came back with our tent.

"Nice try," said Putridity. I leaned over, and I picked up the box that held the Secret of Marriage. That made what's-his-name point the pistol at me. My arms started to shake. But I held on to that box. I said, "This is something personal."

"Give it to me," said the Unnamable.

"No," I said. He pointed that pistol in my face. I hugged my box tighter and said, "No."

"Let him have it," said Henry. "It's probably his pacifier."

"It's my medicine," I said. "I get severe asthma attacks."

"Let him have it," said Henry.

"I wouldn't want you to stop breathing," said the Devil, pointing the gun right at my left eye. My left eye was burning, and I think I was crying, but I held on to the Secret of Marriage. The Devil smiled like a little kid who's just walked into Disneyworld. Todd moved his feet, and Wool Cap turned, pointed the gun at Todd, and his grin got even bigger.

Then he put Todd's Lowe pack (that he'd just gotten the Christmas before) on his back and fired a shot into the air.

"Don't even try to follow us," he said. "We know where you live." He tried to laugh, but it sounded more like a cough to me.

Henry had already walked away, like he didn't want to watch. We could hear them arguing as they disappeared into the trees, down a trail that led back toward the houses.

SEVEN

Todd didn't say a thing — and I knew that was bad. Nothing is scarier than when he's really, really quiet. The way he moved scared me, too. He walked quickly, just like a tiger in a zoo. He just about ran up the tree, tore the tent fly off, and came back and stuffed it in my pack.

"It's something," I said.

"I put the knife in my pants. And I've got my wallet, and one can of chili."

"And my pack," I said, and then made the mistake of keeping going. I said, "And my fishing line!" like that was the most thrilling news in the world. Todd gave me a look that made me feel like a . . . you know what.

He grabbed my pack, threw the chili into it, stuck it on his back, and started walking, so fast I had to jog to keep up. He made it as far as the first big tree. I can still see that tree. It was the kind with bark that looks like camouflage, some dark, some light, in patches. He made it to that tree, and then he yelled, this horrible noise, and then he punched the tree with all his strength.

His face turned slightly purple, and his mouth opened like he couldn't breathe. The look on his face was mostly just amazed. Then he screamed. It's a scary thing to hear your big brother scream like that. It's not supposed to happen.

Todd has a lot of strength. His fingers looked like they were attached wrong — I could tell already. I ran up to him, but he was still hopping around and screaming, and I couldn't even look at his hand until he sat down and started to cry.

"I'll kill him," he said, "if it's the last thing I do, I'll come back here and take that gun from him and stick it in his mouth and pull the trigger! I swear!"

"Todd . . ." I said, and maybe it was the wrong time to say this, but I said, "Maybe we should go to the hospital."

"No WAY!" he screamed. "We're getting there! We're finishing this trip! I don't care if my hand is broken! We're going to Dad's house and we're not going to let that — *that* — that stop us."

But he was still crying. I just stroked his hand a

little. He said, "It was a .22 pistol, Worm! I could have rushed him. He never would have fired. Even if he had, it was just a .22! It wouldn't have even hurt that much!"

I was thinking, what if he shot you in the face, but I had enough good sense at this point not to say anything. Todd said:

"I can't believe I let him do it! I'm sorry, Worm . . ."

"We're going to be OK," I said, even though I had no idea what we were going to eat or where we were going to sleep, and we still had two nights' walk ahead. I patted Todd's shoulder. It was a strange feeling. For a second, it must have looked like I was older than he was, but I sure didn't feel older. I didn't have much to give, but I still wanted to.

After a while, he stood up. His hand was already turning strange colors. I knew from the way he walked that it must have hurt like a hundred rabies shots. But he just started walking down the creek. It was still broad daylight, of course, but we couldn't care.

And then I spotted it. I didn't even know it was mine, right away. I actually thought, who would have hung a squirrel from a tree? And then I realized. I whooped, and Todd turned around and looked at me like my hair had just turned blue, and watched me jump and skip over to that squirrel and hold it up and shout:

"Dinner!"

He couldn't even think what questions to ask. He walked over, and touched the squirrel like he wanted to make sure it wasn't a rubber squirrel I'd hidden in my pack. Then he said, "You caught it?"

Of course, he didn't even know I'd tried to do it. I said, with complete and utter modesty, like a Super Bowl quarterback with champagne in his hair:

"I just followed the directions in my book."

"Wow," Todd said. He actually *said* that. "Wow." I untied the slipknot and Todd held the limp squirrel in his hands. Its mouth was slightly open, so you could see its big front teeth. It looked a little surprised. Todd carried it a little ways toward the creek, stopped, and said, "I've still got the matches in my pocket. The ones I used yesterday."

"And you've got the knife."

"We've got one can of chili. We could make sort of a stew."

"Yummy!"

"Does it say anything in your book about how to make a browse bed?"

"Probably."

"And we still have the tent fly," he said, more or less talking to himself now. "That's our cover."

"And my fishhooks," I reminded him.

"But the main thing now is to walk," Todd announced.

"But," I said, "if we walk until it's dark — and

then make a fire — isn't it going to be real obvious where we are? I mean, fires are less obvious in the daytime."

"That's true," said Todd. He nodded, and actually considered my opinions. "Maybe we should quit a little before sunset. Let's walk until then anyway." He rubbed his hand and made a face.

"Agreed," I said. I put my book and the Secret of Marriage in the pack on his back, and I started off ahead of him.

It's weird, but as I walked alongside the creek, I actually felt good. No. I felt great.

I started thinking of a typical morning at home, when I had to remember my lunch, and if I'd done my science homework, and where I'd left it, and where I'd left my sneakers, and had I played basketball yesterday (which meant they were probably in the bathroom) or had I not (which meant they were probably in the bedroom), and whether or not it was a gym day (which would mean I'd need my shorts), and was I meeting Ken after school (which meant I'd need my card collection), and on and on.

But now, in the woods, it seemed like everything I needed could fit into a daypack: my rope, my fishhooks, one can of chili, and the Secret of Marriage. Well, there was the tent fly too, but if it didn't rain we wouldn't even need that. True, we weren't exactly going to get fat on the squirrels I could catch, and who knew if I was even going to catch another one, and I wasn't exactly sure what we were going to wrap ourselves up in to sleep that night. But I thought we'd figure it out. We'd think of something. I swung my arms and marched down that trail.

The creek was running in its usual slow easy way right there, and as we walked there started to be more woods along it. After a little while you couldn't see any houses, and the dirt trail we'd been following pretty much disappeared, which I thought was a good sign. It meant we had to beat our way through this raspy kind of grass that scratched you a little when you brushed against it, and once or twice we ran into thorn-thickets that were too nasty and we cut around them. But it was beautiful there. It felt like some new land we'd discovered. I didn't need to pretend we were explorers or woodsmen entering the new world. We *were* woodsmen, and even if it wasn't exactly the new world, it sure felt like wilderness. There were birds everywhere, some I knew (like bluejays and cardinals), and a whole bunch that I didn't know, and I thought they must be birds that were native only to this stretch of Accomack Creek. The trees looked different, bigger and older, and I saw a humongous fly with red wings and I told Todd, "Look at that!" But he didn't say anything. I wanted to keep yelling, "Look at that vine!" "Look at that blue stone!" "I wonder where that trail goes?" "Don't the cicadas sound different here?" but Todd kept his head down. I couldn't exactly blame him. But one thing I love more than anything is new trails. If they're new I can always imagine they lead to something amazing that I've never seen before, like an old quarry, or an open field, or a cave that dwarfs live in, or a beautiful girl in a white dress who lives in a tree. Now I had a new trail under my boots and I was first in line.

I started thinking about the first time we ever went camping with Dad. It was in the backyard. Mom came out to tuck us in before we went to sleep. She even brought out ice cream for dessert. I was maybe seven years old, and it sure seemed like an adventure to me. I remembered how dark it was, and how faraway the house seemed, and how in the dark our backyard suddenly became mysterious. I was scared, but I was in between Dad and Todd, who was a big nine. It would have been nice if, after all this struggle to get somewhere, we knew that Dad had a tent ready in the backyard, and a fire burning, and ice cream for dessert. But things hadn't been that simple for a long time anyway.

One time — I was in fifth grade — Dad took Todd and me camping. Up in the Shenandoah, up at Big Meadows. We saw a snake catch a fish one day; it was a fantastic trip. We got back and Mom was like cold rain — just her face — was like freezing cold rain. Because she'd just found out that Dad had forgotten to do the taxes the year before. I guess the Internal Revenue Service hadn't caught up with them for a whole year, so that meant they owed even more than if they'd gotten caught sooner. It was a lot of money. Mom said how much, and Dad sat down on the stool at the counter where I ate my Pop Tarts every morning. He has this kind of tall thin head, and he always sits up real straight. But that day, it seemed like his head was too heavy for him. He didn't say anything. He just laid his head down on the counter. And that was the end of our trip. Sometimes trips can keep going for a few days after you get home, if you can sort of hang on to the feeling of them. Not that one. Dad wouldn't get up to go to work the next day. Mom was screaming at him, and she stopped only because she had to go to work.

I didn't know what it was, but I knew Dad had a good reason for being up on that roof.

We covered some ground before Todd said, "Let's quit. We've got a lot to do," and I said, "Yeah, we've got a lot to do."

We had no idea. We picked a spot on a little rise, where there were three silver trees in sort of a half circle, and we got the top of the tent fly tied to their branches and the bottom weighted down with rocks so it was pretty much over our heads. I wouldn't have wanted to sit out a thunderstorm in it, though. It was hard for Todd to help, with his hand all swollen up. He got out his knife and tried skinning the squirrel, but he could hardly squeeze the handle without its hurting so bad he had to yell. We consulted my book and decided it wouldn't be too hard to make a browse bed (what else were we going to sleep in?), but with the bad hand it turned out Todd couldn't do much there either. I was the one who had to wander through the woods looking for pine trees, because the book said evergreens were your wisest choice since they had the springiest branches. I think the guy who wrote the book must have lived in Vermont or somewhere. His pictures showed all these spruces and firs, but you never see those kinds of trees where I live except in the 7-Eleven parking lot at Christmas time.

I had to walk about half a mile to find some pine trees. There was a whole group of them, on the rise, all in a row like someone had planted them there. I stood in front of them and said, "I'd like to borrow some branches please." Only it seemed like the trees weren't too crazy about it. It was hard pulling the branches off. You can't pull straight out, of course; you have to kind of peel them. But it seemed like I'd get them almost off and then they'd really get determined to stay on and I'd end up having to twist the branches, with all the needles turning in my face, until it would finally tear off. It must have taken me an hour to get enough for a bed, and I was tired when I was done. I mean, when I thought I was done.

I had to drag all those branches back to our campsite; that took a few trips. And it turned out Todd was having a hard time finding enough firewood. Since we'd had that big rain, you couldn't take just any branches, because those lying on the ground were still pretty wet. You had to look for some that were stuck up in the trees, or, best of all, dead trees that were about ready to come down but weren't too rotten. We had to be super choosy, because we only had one pack of matches. And we didn't have any paper or anything to start the fire with. We got lucky there, though. Todd walked along the creek and found this spot where the bank had caved in a little. There was a snag under the bank, a place where driftwood had gotten stuck, and a whole pile of dead leaves were caught against it. The creek had dropped since the leaves and wood got caught there, so none of it was wet, and, since the bank had caved in, it even had a sort of dirt roof overhead, so the rain didn't hit it much. Todd stood in the creek up to his thighs, and scooped those leaves with one hand up to me, on the bank, and I carried them like they were Mom's china, or my collection of 1969 rookie cards. I don't think I lost a single leaf.

So Todd got the fire going with one hand (he had the other wrapped up in a T-shirt) while I tried to skin the squirrel. I went by the book of course, ha ha. That book already had its cover off and most of its pages dirty. Guess it was a good buy at four ninety-five.

The book said to make an incision behind the ankles first. I held that dead squirrel in my hands, and looked at its ankles, and looked at its eyes. You expect to see something meaningful in dead eyes, but there's nobody home. I can't explain what it is you see in living eyes that tells you there's a . . . I guess a *soul*, there. But I can tell you, you don't see it in dead eyes. And I couldn't help thinking about that squirrel getting strangled on its way down from its nest. Just on its way to check out a pile of acorns somewhere, and BAM! Did it have time to feel surprised? Or scared?

I said my Indian thanks to it, but just in my head, because what if Todd thought it was dumb?

What you do when you skin a squirrel is, you make a cut behind the ankles and then you peel. You get your fingers into that greasy space between the skin and the muscle and you pull. And then when you've got enough off, you get a big bunch of it in your hand and pull harder. It comes off right over the squirrel's head, inside out, just like a sweater. The hard part is keeping the fur off the skin. I didn't do so hot with that the first time. I had a hard time getting the skin off over the head, so I was wrestling with it, and getting the fur on my greasy hands, and then getting fur on the meat when I touched that, and when I was done it looked like someone had felt sorry for it and tried to put its fur back on even though the skin was off.

But I cut it up with the knife and spread the fly on the ground and set the chunks of meat there, and meanwhile Todd got a nice fire going. So I went to work making a bed for us, while Todd started cooking dinner, which was a serious challenge since we had no pots. The Creature had taken them. I wondered if maybe he'd thrown half our stuff in the sewer on his way home. But I didn't think about it for more than one second.

Todd solved the pot problem by waiting until the fire burned down to coals, and then he just stuck the whole can of chili in the coals with the label peeled off. It took a while for the fire to burn down, but by then I had a sort of kind of bed made. I tried to interweave the branches, the way the book said, but they didn't always want to interweave. Some of them just kept springing loose, and in the end what we had for a bed was more like a big heap of pine branches. I lay down on it and Todd said, "What does it feel like?"

"It feels like . . ."

"Come on," he said.

"It feels like I'm lying on baseball bats."

"This is crazy," he said. "I can't believe we're doing this."

I started to laugh. I just started to — and right then, perfect timing, along came a guy walking his dog. An old guy, wearing these baggy shorts like old retired guys always wear, even though his legs were very hairy. Completely covered with gray and white hair. He had one of those white sun hats on, the kind with the floppy brim, and he was walking a poodle with a pom-pom on the end of its tail. He walked right by us, just strolling through the woods. As he passed, he looked at us, waved, and said, "Good afternoon." I think we both just sat there and stared at him for a minute before Todd finally said, "Hi."

Good thing we weren't standing next to the fire. As soon as he was out of sight we started laughing so hard we would have fallen in. Todd was actually crying when he sat up straight again. Then he said, "Well. Let's have dinner!" and we both started howling again. Finally I had to walk away from our camp to quit giggling. And still, while we were eating, every time I looked at Todd I'd start laughing and almost spit out my food.

But when you have one can of chili and one squirrel between two people, you do not spit out your food.

We roasted the squirrel hunks over the coals —

they cooked fine. We used sharpened sticks. Todd asked me what they tasted like, and when I said, "Like chicken, actually," he smiled. We'd both had this teacher at school, Mr. Marks, who was really cool and liked to try out all kinds of strange food, like rattlesnakes and frogs' legs. He'd tell kids about them in class, and whenever we asked him what they tasted like, he'd say, "Like chicken, actually." Finally, one time Todd said, "Then why don't you just eat chicken?"

I said, "What are we going to cook with from now on?"

He pointed at the chili can.

I said, "Remember the time we went camping with Dad and he forgot to bring shorts along so he took an ax and made his jeans into cutoffs?"

"Sure," Todd said, "I remember."

The squirrel was gone. I held my stick in the coals until it started to flame. I said, "What did one candle say to the other?"

"Worm," Todd said. "Remember the time Dad disappeared for a week?"

"That's when I first started being afraid they'd split up."

"Do you know what he did?"

"He said he went and stayed in a motel on the Eastern Shore."

"And stayed in bed for seven days straight."

"Was he sick?" I said, even though I knew what Todd was talking about.

"Sick up here," Todd said, tapping the side of his head. "I think he had a breakdown. I heard Mom talking about it on the phone."

"So you think Dad's crazy?"

Todd snorted. "Sitting up on a roof for — what is it, five days now? You don't think that's crazy?"

"Then what are we going to get him for?" I jumped up and threw the stick into the fire. "If he's so totally nuts, if he's just a complete basket case, why don't we let him rot up there?"

"I thought you knew about all this," Todd said.

"All what?"

"That Dad has breakdowns." Todd had this D–U–M–B smile on his kisser that made we want to poke a burning stick in his face. "I think that's why he lost his job."

"You *think*! You keep saying you think. Maybe you think wrong. Is that possible?"

"Yes, it is, Worm, but not on this one. You know it, too, if you think about it. Think about the way Dad acts sometimes."

I jumped up and walked off into the woods. You know why? Because I was afraid I might hit Todd. That would have been the first time I'd hit him in my entire life, I mean, not counting when I was four or something. I didn't want to start a serious fight when we had to depend on each other, but God I hated him right then.

Why did Dad lose his job, and have to leave the house sometimes? I think he just got sad. I think that was the problem. I think some days he just got too sad to deal with things. And I knew how that was.

His being sad didn't blot out the card games he'd play with us almost every day when he came home from work. Almost every day. Or the times he took us way deep into the woods to see something special — and it turned out it was a rotten log that he said was fine compost for his garden. See, I knew deep down that he was great. And Todd acted like he wasn't so sure about it. That's why I was really so mad at Todd.

I didn't figure all this out until I'd walked about a mile into the woods, in the dark. I loved the way the woods smelled at night, in the summer, that cooling-down smell. So I sat awhile. The bugs were cheeping, not too loud because it was only June, but the gnats and mosquitoes were gone, thank God. The woods smelled sweet almost, like all the heat that had soaked into them all day was rising up out of them like a kind of sweet steam. I wanted to sit there all night, sit there and hate Todd's guts.

I had to cut back over to the creek and follow it

upstream to find our camp again. It was easy to spot in the dark because the coals were still glowing. When I got there Todd said, “Where have you been? We’ve got to make time tonight.”

“Thinking,” I told him. “I’ve been thinking.”

“Think as you walk,” he said.

There was a clear, sandy trail along the side of the creek, and the walking was nice. I was beat, because I hadn’t slept during the day, the way we were supposed to. I just kept slogging along, looking at my feet, sometimes up at the trees, whose branches were the only things you could see in the dark because the sky was brighter than the woods. The outlines of the tree branches made it seem a little less spooky and lonely. I felt really lonely that night. Todd might as well not have been there.

We passed under a highway bridge and came to a stretch where the creek was just a ditch with concrete slopes for its banks. At the top of the slope on one side was a chainlink fence, and behind the fence was a Doberman who came over and snarled at us. I think he was protecting a junkyard. We passed an apartment tower that looked like a skyscraper. It was built right up against the creek, and there were lights on in some of the apartments. We could even see a couple of people out on a balcony, and I thought they were looking right at us. I sort of crouched as I walked — like that was going to hide me. We could see them plain as day, holding their drinks in little plastic cups, and I thought I could even hear what they were saying — something about, "Marcia's not normal." We could hear music playing from some other apartment somewhere. I guess they all had their sliding glass balcony doors open.

After a couple of hours my head hurt from just plain being tired, my stomach hurt maybe because it wasn't used to squirrel, and my feet hurt because the pinky-toe on my left foot kept getting jammed against the inside of the boot and scraped until every step was like rubbing it with steel wool. But I could not — would not — say a word about it to Todd. So I started making up poems. That's what I do when even a joke isn't enough. I made this up:

> A boy named Worm
> Felt like a germ
> And wanted to see his Mommy.
> He dreamed of hot cocoa
> Until he went loco
> Oh what a sad boy was he.

Don't worry, I wasn't planning on getting them published. It just made me forget about my pinky-toe.

There once was a boy named Todd
Whose backbone was stiff as a rod.
He said "Yes I can.
For I'm a true man.
Just check out my beautiful bod."

There was one spot where the concrete bank got so steep that we had to hike along the top of the slope, on a little strip of cement up against a fence. On the other side of the fence was a big supermarket that was open even though it was the middle of the night. I tried to read Todd's mind. Was it safe to try to go shopping? Todd still had some money. But it seemed like it would be chicken to even talk about it. And Todd never said a word. We passed by that supermarket and left it there glowing in the middle of its twenty acres of parking lot.

A creek in the woods
Went where it should
never steer.
It flowed past the highways
and Worm said my days
are weird.

And not long after that:

A creek that goes through a tunnel, I think,
Becomes very useful as a link

From one side of a road to the other.
But to people walking through, it seems
To go on and on like a stinky dream
Until you want to kill your big brother.

I swear there were things under our feet in that tunnel. We tied our boots onto our backpacks to wade through. I know I stepped on at least one dead rat. Maybe it was a mouse. A little later I felt some glass with my toes, and stepped someplace else, but that could have been it for my foot. Major gash. The water was up to my thighs. So the next time we came to one of those tunnels we climbed up over it and ran across an eight-lane highway with our heads down, hiding in the median strip, with all those headlights glaring right on us — all we needed was a ball and chain. When we got to the other side, I said to Todd, "Feel like going out?" and he said, "What?"

"What did one candle say to the other," I said, "remember?"

"No."

"'Feel like going out?' Get it? Ha ha ha. Listen, did you figure out the one about Friday yet?"

"Did you stop being mad at me?" Todd said.

"I guess so," I said.

I wish Todd had said something else right then. Something like: "Good," or "I'm glad," or best of all: "How're you feeling?" Usually he was great about asking stuff like that, but now, I think his hand and his brain were hurting so much he didn't have time to ask anyone except himself how they were feeling.

So I asked him. "How're you feeling?" He said, "OK."

EIGHT

Finally we found some trees, and the creek came out of its concrete ditch. I guess we went on for a couple of hours after that. Maybe more, because all I remember is slogging along a gravel path until sunrise started. All you could see was the sky starting to glow a teeny bit, but I was beat, and I voted to stop, and Todd agreed. We came to another highway bridge and just decided to set up our camp under it. It was a little bridge, but there was a kind of shelf at the top of the concrete rise underneath where you could lie down and touch the steel beams. And just past the bridge were woods. I figured I could set some snares there, and try to fish a little bit. We wouldn't have any breakfast, but maybe we could get lunch. Didn't seem like anyone would see us under there.

So I set out with the knife to get some bedding. Todd's hand was pretty bad. He kept stroking it and petting it with his good hand and biting his lip. I cut through a patch of stumpy little trees and climbed over a pile of chopped-up tree trunks and branches, and found a park — grills and picnic tables and a blacktop road. I just decided I wouldn't worry about it. We were so far from home, who would even know about two kids from Colonial Park who ran away? Across the blacktop road was a bunch of pines, so I headed over there and started tearing and pulling off branches. God, it was a lot of work. And I had to rush because it was really getting to be daylight. I was so hungry I could have eaten an entire can of black olives. And I despise olives. They make me want to puke.

I was swearing at those pine branches by the time I got an armful. I hauled them back to the bridge, and we sort of stuffed them up where the concrete shelf was. Of course there wasn't enough. I was so mad at Todd for punching that tree and making me do all the work, I could have punched a tree. I hauled myself back to the pines while he sat there stroking his hand, and I twisted off more branches, and I dragged them back. Then I went back again and scouted around until I found a good squirrel tree, and set a snare just like the last one. It wasn't too hard finding a squirrel tree. The squirrels in that park looked as fat and sassy as housecats. Then I went back to my pine-branches bed, and tried to snuggle down into it, with my dirty, sweaty Wolverine T-shirt and my wet smelling-like-creekwater checkered shorts still on. Todd was already asleep. But I couldn't stand the way I smelled, so I took off my clothes. The pine-needles were tickling me, and the branches were digging into my ribs and my hip, and some pine sap from one branch was getting onto my knee, and I wondered if we wouldn't have been better off just sleeping on the cement. But I fell asleep fast. That's how rundown I was.

It was hot when I woke up, but dark. I thought I'd slept all the way till night until I saw the clouds overhead. A big storm was blowing in, which I thought would be good in a way, because nobody would be around in the rain. I got my clothes on and found my fishing line. Todd was still asleep, with his face covered over with pine needles and his injured hand sticking out from the branches, set very carefully on the concrete. It was blue and reddish-black and puffed up twice the size it should have been.

Bait was easy. I just dug with a rock in the dirt until I found some worms. They were all up near the surface, since we'd just had that other big rain. My father always said they didn't feel much pain, but how did he know? Had he ever asked a worm? They always squirmed and wiggled when you put them on the hook.

But, too bad, I needed to eat right now. I hooked that worm twice to make sure he'd stay, and tossed my line into Accomack Creek.

I wrapped the fishing line around my hand, since the one thing I didn't want to do was hook a big fish and have it swim off with my line. There were a lot of carp in that creek, and sometimes you could catch a catfish. The carp were pretty easy to catch, but there was one problem with them: they fed on all the junk in the bottom of the creek, and nobody ever ate them because their gills and their bodies were all full of muck. You had to clean them really carefully. But how choosy was I going to be now? I stood there on the edge of the creek and dreamed about French toast, steaming, butter dripping off the edges.

I was standing there dreaming about cheeseburgers when I felt a tug on the line and fell over headfirst into the water.

I guess some of the reasons why people invented fishing poles hadn't occurred to me. A big fish can pull pretty hard, and the pole is made to absorb some of that weight, which is why you reel in the line. So how exactly was I supposed to reel in this fish when it was attached to my hand? It wasn't strong enough to drag me through the water or anything, and I got back on my feet, but — yow! — every time that thing swam away, the line felt like it was going to slice through my hand. I started running down the side of the creek, kicking up big splashes of water, sprinting through the scratchy grass that grew there. If I couldn't pull that carp in, I was going to wear him out. Even though my hand was turning red, I was not going to let that thing go.

"YΛΛΛΛH" I yelled, mostly out of pure being-mad-at-myself, not caring who heard — but someone heard.

The someone was standing right behind me, and when he whispered, "Want some help?" I jumped so high I could have slam-dunked a basketball.

The guy took a stick and wrapped the line around it, and pulled on the stick. I could have slapped him. I mean, why couldn't I have thought of that?

But I controlled myself. I said, "Thank you."

He was a strange-looking guy. He had these dreadlocks — like those reggae guys from Jamaica have — except he definitely was not from Jamaica. His dreadlocks were blond, and his face was as white as a brand-new sheet of Xerox paper. He was so skinny it made you worried to look at him, and he was wearing a white shirt. White was not his color, I decided as I looked at him. There was ketchup on his shirt, there was grease, there may even have been some blood. Somehow I had the feeling it wasn't necessarily his blood. Definitely a black-shirt kind of guy.

He pulled in my fish. It was about a foot long. It lay there in the scratchy grass, gasping, until my new friend took a stick, raised it way back, high over his head, and brought it down as hard as he could on the carp's head. The carp quit gasping.

"Pleased to meet you," he said, holding out his hand. "Name's Ricardo."

And I'm José, I thought — this guy looked about as Spanish as Todd did. I said:

"Hi. I'm José." I swear it just popped out of my mouth.

"Cool," he said. Then I realized we were standing next to a pup tent. I'd been so busy with the fish, I'd never even seen the tent.

"You live here?" I said.

"In the summers. It's nice. There's a bus straight into town."

"Which town?"

"D.C."

"Oh."

"You from here?"

"I'm from upstream," I said. It sounded silly, but that really was all I knew about where I was or where I was from. I was downstream of Colonial

Park. And I guess closer to Washington than I'd thought.

"What are you doing in my fair park?"

"I ran away," I told him, and then I thought — shut up! Why was I telling this guy all these things? Maybe he was the sort of person who kidnapped runaways and tortured them. Maybe he was already figuring how he could jump me. Did he have a knife in his pocket, did he have a rope in his tent, did he have bodies buried in remote spots all around the Washington area?

"You ran away but you forgot to bring food?" he said.

"It's a long story," I told him. "But we're doing OK." I was looking at that fish, not even really wondering what it would taste like — just wishing it was in my stomach.

"I've got a knife," said Ricardo. He walked over to his tent and came back with a serrated kitchen knife, and proceeded to clean that fish. It was awesome, watching someone who actually knew what he was doing with a fish. When my friends and I caught fish out of Accomack, we usually took them home and buried them in Dad's azalea patch to make the azaleas grow better. Ricardo just took out the gills, and pulled the bones out like they were one piece, which anyone who's ever cleaned a carp can tell you, they are not, and *bam*, he had hunks of carp spread out on a plastic tarp he'd pulled from his tent.

"Split it with you?" he said, and I nodded yes. That wasn't exactly what I had in mind, but what could I say — he'd caught the thing, really, and cleaned it too. But I couldn't believe it when he just popped a piece into his mouth. "Like sushi," he said. "Go ahead."

I looked at the greasy, damp fish chunks, each one leaking a little blood. I looked at Ricardo. It hadn't killed him. Yet.

I squatted down with my butt toward the bushes behind Ricardo's tent. So in case he tried to stab me with the knife, I could run. Then I grabbed a chunk and threw it into my mouth.

When I bit down on it, it crunched. Guess even Ricardo couldn't get all the dirt out of a carp. It didn't taste kind of like chicken. It just tasted very fishy.

I threw another hunk in my mouth, and swallowed as fast as I could. Ricardo and I got into this thing of you pop a piece I pop a piece and before I could think that much about Todd, the fish was gone.

"You look half-starved," said Ricardo. "Want to go to McDonald's?"

"Sorry," I said. "I really can't. Thanks for the fish." I was walking backwards as I talked. "I've got to go find my brother," I said, and then thought, no!

You don't want him to know about Todd! I bumped into a bush and almost fell into it and Ricardo said, "You don't have to be scared of little old me."

I straightened up and looked at his sunburnt nose, and noticed the Captain Planet ring on his finger. I took one step back into that bush and said:

"Are you a homeless person?"

He laughed. "I don't exist," he told me. "I don't pay taxes, I don't take food stamps, I don't go to their evil, soul-killing shelters, and no census worker has come out here to ask me about my housing situation."

"Oh," I said.

"But once a poll-taker came here to ask me if I felt the tax exemption for personal aircraft ought to be cut."

"Really?"

Ricardo cracked up, and I would have felt stupid except he laughed in such a nice way. It wasn't at me.

"I don't need any handouts. A man can live by his wits if he wants to."

"Yeah?"

"And if you're not too squeamish. So. Care to go to McDonald's?"

"No, thanks," I said. "I've got to go." I waved with my fingers. "Thanks for the fish," I said, and when I thought I'd walked far enough away from him, I ran back to our bridge.

Todd was still asleep. I sat right next to him, with

my arms around my knees, and overhead was the sound of cars shooting past. The sky was like a big dark sheet up above, but quiet. I couldn't hear the thunder but I knew it was coming. I knew I ought to sleep, but I still wasn't sleepy. I was thinking about what if Ricardo found our hideout there. I was thinking what if he *was* just a funny-looking, lonesome, homeless person?

Then I saw him walking past the tree where I'd set my snare. I was sitting in a nice lookout spot.

I was dying to know where he was going. Would McDonald's actually let a person like him in? Or was he going to some secret rendezvous with his gang of murderers and child-snatchers? Or was he going to go blow bubbles and dance on a street corner somewhere?

I wouldn't have decided to follow him except for the fact that he was headed toward the highway. I figured, over there, even if he assaulted me, there'd be gas stations and places I could run to. I would have woken Todd up, but, I don't know — I guess I was into doing things by myself now.

I waited until Ricardo was out of sight. Then I climbed down the hill that sloped off the bridge, and crept along through the park, running from tree to tree and picnic table to picnic table, just like a . . . like a guy in an old Army movie, actually. I felt better when I spotted Ricardo walking down the shoulder of the highway. Then I knew he hadn't snuck around behind me.

There was enough tall stuff growing along the side of the road that I could hide behind it and keep an eye on Ricardo. Too bad a lot of it was thistles and baby pine trees. But I was getting curiouser and curiouser. Ricardo just kept on walking down the shoulder of the road, swinging his arms, like he had an appointment somewhere.

We came to an intersection and a gas station that had little pennants strung up for its grand opening. Cruddy cover for me, though. Ricardo walked past the pumps and waved "Hi" to a guy working in the garage. I waited until Ricardo was on the other side of the intersection, and then I walked past the pumps, too, my skin feeling all tingly like a million eyes were on me. I watched Ricardo's back as he crossed the intersection and climbed up a culvert on the other side — I just kept staring at it. If I was really brave, I thought, and just stared straight at him, he'd never ever turn around. But then I got stuck waiting for a lot of traffic to pass, and I watched Ricardo march along the side of the road past another gas station and a Dairy Queen, getting splattered by some rain leaking from the clouds — just drops — and disappear behind the post of a twenty-foot–tall KFC sign.

When I finally got across that intersection I ran up to the pole of the KFC sign and hid behind it.

But no Ricardo. Just a Dunkin Donuts, and a dry cleaners, and a McDonald's. And about fifteen-hundred cars and trucks rolling down that road past me. I wondered what they thought about a skinny kid in very dirty checkered shorts sneaking through the little bushes in front of the Dunkin Donuts.

McDonald's was my goal. Was he going to rob it? Was his gang going to meet there, have some Chicken McNuggets, and pick out which kids they wanted to kidnap from the play area? He'd asked me to go there. What for?

I crouched beside the dry cleaners, and when the traffic going past the drive-up slowed down, I scurried across the lane and plastered myself against the wall beside the drive-up window. I crawled along the side of the building and got pebbles stuck in my knees and hands and came to the windows and slowly, very slowly, stood up and peered inside. A guy with mirrored sunglasses came out the door and stopped and stared at me, but I pretended I was invisible. I crawled through the little bushes they'd planted in white gravel, all the way over to the other side. This time I got little pieces of gravel stuck to my hands and knees. I got up on my knees and peered in the windows.

Then I turned my head and spotted him. Out back. There was a wooden fence, the kind that looks like it's made from a whole bunch of wooden stakes stuck side by side, that made two sides of a square and closed off a corner of the parking lot. Ricardo climbed over it and disappeared. I crouched and ran at the same time (not easy) and when I got to that fence I grabbed hold of the crossbar that held all those stakes together, and peeked over the top, and there he was — fishing around in the Dumpster! His arm was way down deep in garbage, and when he pulled it out, he was holding a Big Mac box. I couldn't believe it when he opened the box and ate about half the burger in one bite.

"Hi, José," he said. "Want some?"

I fell down.

"Don't be a stranger," he called over the fence. "Come share a Happy Meal with me."

I pulled myself back up on the crossbar so I could ask Ricardo a question.

"How did you see me?"

"Back in the park, José. When you were hiding behind those picnic tables, you shouldn't have been in such a hurry." I must have looked shocked, because he went on and told me, in a nice voice, "I may look crazy, but I'm crazy like a hyena. Burger?"

"No, thanks," I said.

"Look," he said. "McDonald's doesn't just throw out garbage." He boosted himself up so he could peer inside the bin. I pulled myself up, swung my legs over the fence and landed so hard my knees shook. Ricardo handed me something. I took it, and then I looked around to see if anyone was watching. When I looked back at my hands, I realized I was holding a Quarter-Pound cheeseburger. Still in the box.

"It's one shift old," Ricardo said, "so they toss it. But it ain't garbage."

He rooted around in there, and when he came out his hands didn't smell like roses. "Want some fries?" he said. "They sort of got scattered around."

I shook my head. Ricardo said, "Hold this for me," and he handed me a chicken fajita. Still in the wrapper. Then he hopped down from the dumpster and I handed it back to him, and he ate it in two bites.

We walked across the McDonald's parking lot, and I opened the box and took a good look at that old cold burger, and listened to my stomach, and took a chomp. But then my conscience started talking and I only took one more bite. Because I had to save some for Todd.

"Time for dessert," said Ricardo.

"You live like this all the time?"

"Freedom," he said. "I've got my freedom. So do you now, I guess."

"I'm going back home."

"What for?"

"Actually," I said, "I'm on a mission." I didn't want him to think I was one of those kids who hate their parents and run away and end up on Fourteenth Street in D.C.

"Don't tell me — a mission from God."

"No. My father's been sitting on the roof of his house for about five days now."

"Sounds like an interesting role model."

"I'm going there to . . . help him." I felt empty, in my chest, for a minute. You know how sometimes your chest or your stomach remembers a bad memory before your brain does, and they tell your brain it's coming even though your brain doesn't know what the bad thought is? Then my brain remembered my bad thought. It was: what exactly were we going to do when we got there?

"I went crazy once, too," Ricardo said. "Tried to kill myself on my twenty-fifth birthday."

"How old are you now?"

"Thirty-three. It turned out I was manic-depressive."

"Were you manic about being depressed or depressed about being manic?"

"Hey! I'll have to remember that one . . . no, it means you have these mood swings, like — mooooooooooood swiiiiiiings. Like, you love the world one second and you want to die the next. But it's all physical. Everything mental is really physical. They treated me with lithium and now I'm normal. Whoops! Here's dessert!"

Dessert was in the trash bin behind the Dunkin

Donuts. Ricardo asked me if I wanted to try looking for myself, but I shook my head. I felt sort of embarrassed when he dug in there and found a creme-filled doughnut still wrapped up in tissue paper and gave it to me. I kept thinking, what if Ken drove up here with his parents right now?

I ate half the doughnut, and walked back down the highway next to Ricardo, holding my burger and half a doughnut in one hand. I ran across that intersection behind Ricardo, even though traffic was coming, and watched him wave to that same guy in the garage. The sky was even darker, and that wind let you know the storm would be coming soon.

I said, "What's the name again of the stuff you take?"

"Lithium," said Ricardo. "It's my one connection to the workaday world. Every Wednesday, I take a bus into town and see my shrink."

"You do? What does he say?"

"Not much. He's a shrink. Oh, you mean about my lifestyle? He's very nonjudgmental. Whoa! There's tonight's dinner. See how easy it is?"

I wondered for a minute what he was talking about. Even though I was looking right at a dead raccoon by the side of the road. I still couldn't believe my eyes when he picked it up by the tail and sniffed it.

"You get so you can tell just by looking at them how old they are," Ricardo said. "Anyway, we know it wasn't here when we came by half an hour ago."

"You're going to eat that?" I said.

"Well, not raw. Coon sushi? I don't think so."

"But it got run over by a car."

He shrugged. "Even lions and grizzly bears scavenge. Don't you watch the Discovery Channel?"

I knew that, logically, he had a point. But all I could think of was, how many cars had gone over that coon? I took a little peek at it, and I decided I really didn't want to share the coon with him. But I did want to tell him something. I said:

"I don't think my father's manic-depressive. I think he's just sad."

"Could be."

"I think sometimes he just gets too sad to deal with everything. He just needs us to show up and remind him he's OK."

"Who's 'us'?"

"What?" I hoped Ricardo couldn't see my Wolverine shirt shaking from my heart pounding. I said, "Oh. Sometimes I say 'us' when I just mean 'me.'" Lame! Lame! Lame!

"Oh," said Ricardo. "OK."

"Don't you get lonely?" I said, to change the subject.

He grinned and nodded, and all his dreadlocks

shook. "Occupational hazard," he said. "I must say I'm very glad I met you today."

"I'm glad I met you."

I felt like I'd actually been useful to him, in some funny way. It was a good feeling.

"But how come your face is so pale?" I said. "Does that come from taking the medicine?"

"No, no," he said. "It's mostly because" — he stuck out his top teeth and raised his arms and made his fingers like claws and tried to talk with a Transylvanian accent — "I only come out at night! Unless I really get hungry."

"Why?"

"Less hassle," he said. "Police tend to take one look at me and get a powerful urge to make an arrest."

"Don't you get hot with your hair like that?"

"Cutting my hair would be compromising," he said in a serious voice, the first serious voice I'd heard him talk in. "I don't compromise."

We were back in the park now. I told him I'd better go see if my fire was out. I can lie like that, just without thinking. It's scary.

"Want to see my latest project first? It's totally cool."

I knew technically I shouldn't go over to his tent, but Ricardo wasn't exactly a stranger anymore. Sometimes I just can't help doing things that I know aren't smart. Plus I had my checkered shorts on, for power. Plus Todd could hear me if I screamed. "Just for a second," I said.

He had a teeny little trail through the thorn bushes over to his tent. We stood next to the creek and he pointed, and I looked, and I saw a big sheet of plywood that looked like it was levitated off the water. Then I looked a little closer, and I saw there were little oil drums attached somehow to the bottom.

"A raft!" I said. "Cool! That is totally cool . . ." My mind was really working, picturing me and Todd with one of those. I could see us floating down the creek like Huck Finn. What an awesome idea!

"Can you show me how to make one?" I said.

"It's hard to scrounge up those little oil drums. But, sure. It's easy if you have the right stuff."

"Cool," I said again, with such awe in my voice it made Ricardo laugh.

"Well," he said, "go check your fire, José."

I came real close to saying, Huh? Then I remembered and I nodded and said, "Right. See you."

But I came running back about two seconds later, yelling, "Look at this!" Ricardo laughed and said, "Cool."

I'd snared another squirrel! I held it way up high over my head and said, "I think I'm actually good at this!"

Ricardo smiled, kind of slowly, in a way that

made me think he got it. He knew why it was so important to me that I could snare squirrels. Right then I wouldn't have thought twice about telling him that my real name wasn't José — I could have even told him why my name was Worm. But I just stood there and soaked in that smile for a moment, and then I waved and said, "'Bye, Ricardo."

I ran back to the bridge and got there just before the storm hit. It was a whopper. Lightning slicing up the sky, and big black thunderheads rumbling, and rain coming down so hard you could hardly see through it. Thank God for our bridge.

NINE

"Where have you been?" Todd said when I climbed up beside him. He didn't sound real mad, so I figured he couldn't have been awake too long. I handed him the burger and the half-a-doughnut and said, "There's more where that came from."

"Where'd you get this?" he said. But he didn't wait for me to answer before he started wolfing it down.

I told him the truth, but he still kept eating. "And we've got this squirrel —" But suddenly I thought of something. As Ricardo and I were coming back to his tent, I'd spotted the nicest pile of firewood. Which was now sitting out there getting soaked.

I took off all my clothes — who was going to see?

I ran through the rain like a maniac, yelling and waving my arms, and grabbed that wood, hugged it to my chest, and ran back under the bridge — and it only took about three seconds total.

"Here," I called up to Todd, "we've got some pretty dry firewood for roasting that squirrel."

I skinned the squirrel and chopped it up, quick as I could because Todd was just squatting there watching. I dumped the meat-chunks on the fly in front of him, my way of saying, "Go ahead." Then I ran up and climbed in among the itchy-scratchy pine branches and rolled around until I felt relatively dry, and got my clothes back on.

Todd went down to the flat space beside the creek, after a while, and got the fire going. He didn't have too hard a time because the rain hadn't really soaked into the wood. I just watched, even though I knew it was hard with one hand. I knew he wanted to do it himself, and besides, it was so cozy lying there, listening to the rain. The air was still warm, and the wind blew itself out after a while but the rain kept coming, beating on the bridge over my head, and I just snuggled up against myself, and before I thought I was going to, I fell asleep.

When I woke up Todd had the squirrel roasted and he'd already eaten his share. The rain had stopped, and a little sunshine was trying to come out. The trees were dripping, the water was coming plop-plop-plop off the edges of the bridge, and there were big brown puddles everywhere.

"We've had some bad luck on this trip," I told Todd when I sat down beside him and started on the squirrel, "but finding this bridge sure was lucky."

He just grunted. I didn't know what he was thinking anymore. I figured that hand was really hurting him, and that was what he mostly had to pay attention to.

"One more day," I said. "Right? One more day to Dad's? Why don't we just get going now? No one's going to be outside after this storm, anyway."

He nodded. "All right," he said. He stood up and started gathering up stuff. It didn't take long, of course.

I really wanted to stop and say goodbye to Ricardo. And then I remembered about my fishing line. I must have left it there after we cleaned out that fish and ate it, so that gave me an excuse. Todd got the pack on his back and we started off down the creek, skirting past the new puddles. Someone called, "Hey!" and we both froze and looked over.

I really and truly did not believe at first that it was Mr. Harris. I thought it had to be someone who looked just like him. I was trying to think what he was doing there — was he a guy who'd had a cookout and left his serving spoon behind and wanted to know if we'd seen it?

"Worm, run!" Todd hollered and *then* I believed it was Mr. Harris. "You boys get back here!" Mr. Harris yelled. "It's time this little charade was over!"

He had us. We couldn't run past him to the park entrance, and even if we did get past him, where we were going to go? We'd be out on the highway. We couldn't swim away from him. Last time it'd been dark and he'd been surprised to see us, but this time we knew he wasn't going to give up so easily. He came running at us, and we went crashing through the scratchy grass alongside the creek, because we didn't know what else to do, and then something amazing happened. I had a brilliant idea.

"This way!" I yelled at Todd, even though we were already going that way. I ran ahead of him, down the teeny path to Ricardo's tent, and grabbed Ricardo's slimy hand. He was skinning the raccoon. "Can we borrow your raft?" I hollered, and he looked at me, looked at Todd, looked toward where Mr. Harris was trying to get through the thorns, and said, "I see you need some help." Then he took his skinning knife and chopped the clothesline that held the raft to shore. "That's all I can do," he said.

"Thank you," I said, "thank you," and Todd and I splashed out onto the raft, which was already starting to float away. Todd grabbed the pole that was lying on the shore, which Ricardo must have made for the raft, and shoved us out into the deep water just before Mr. Harris got through the storms.

He splashed out knee-deep into the water, but we were already floating away from him, fast. The creek was high because of the rain, and this happened to be a spot where the water funneled through a narrow spot past a sandbank. Mr. Harris tried to scramble up on the sandbank, but we were gone before he got to where we'd been, floating out in the middle of the creek, raft spinning around and around, getting away.

He ran down the bank, yelling at us. "Your mother's going nuts, did you know that? You've got to stop this crazy stunt and come home!" Why didn't he swim after us? I wondered. Maybe the current was too strong to swim and grab the raft at the same time?

"Tell her we're OK," Todd called.

"You don't look OK to me," Mr. Harris said.

"We're fine," Todd called. "Tell her we'll talk to her tomorrow."

Mr. Harris kept on jogging along the shore. We really weren't going that fast, and I could tell he was thinking of some way he could come out and get us. But the water was chest-high where we were, at least, and what could he do? Run up ahead of us, stand in the middle of the creek, and try to tip the raft over?

Actually, he could.

And maybe he would. I started to feel not so safe. He was pretty mad. And there was no reason for him to give up. If he kept following us, the creek might hit a narrow place where he could stop us. Or what if we ran up against a log sticking out into the middle of the creek, or what if the creek went into a tunnel and got too shallow for us to float?

"You were on Channel 53!" he yelled. "Everyone is talking about you!"

"How did we do in the track meet?" Todd yelled.

"We stank," called Mr. Harris. "But who cares? I told your mother I was going to get you boys home, and I'm going to do it!"

He scrambled out onto a log that stuck about halfway across the creek. We were headed right for him. This was crazy — he was my big brother's gym teacher! He used to be a teacher at the elementary school and said "Hi" to the kids every morning and called every one of us "Buddy." But Todd was shoving that pole at the water as hard as he could, with one hand. I grabbed it and helped. We just couldn't find the bottom. The current kept kicking the pole away from any grab he could get. The creek was spinning us right toward Mr. Harris, who was crouched on that log ready to jump onto the raft, or snatch one of us.

I guess I'll never know exactly what he had in mind, because Todd grabbed the pole away from me, lay down on the raft on his stomach, ducked his head and shoulders along with his arms with the pole stuck out deep into the water, gave a tremendous push and sent us over toward the far bank of the creek. This gave Mr. Harris only one choice — and he jumped. His splash hit us both, but the current was pulling fast past that log, and by the time Mr. Harris's head came above water, we were downstream. He spluttered and spat out a long stream of creekwater, and his baseball cap floated away.

I would have laughed, but half of me felt bad. He was just trying to help out, in his weird way. Very weird way. I grabbed my stomach and whooped.

"Worm, cut it out! He's not done yet!"

When I looked up, I could see Todd had a point. Mr. Harris was racing down the bank, all two-hundred-fifty gym-hardened thick-bicepped pounds of him. And man, did he look mad! It was like watching a moose charging at you.

"I don't know what he's going to do," Todd said. "Maybe swim out. He's mad enough. I can't hit him with this stick."

"No," I said, "don't do that."

"We better think of *some*thing," Todd said.

"I'll tell you what," I said when I turned to look at where we were going. "DUCK!"

He turned and saw the chainlink fence that was stretched across the creek just in time. We both flattened ourselves against that plywood surface of the raft, but I felt one of those spiky points of the fence scratch my back. I looked up, after a minute, and the first thing I saw was empty ground all around us, no trees except in little clumps. Then I saw Mr. Harris with his nose pressed up against that fence, looking as mad and sorry as a kid who's just had Christmas canceled. The creekbank had caved in on one side, under the fence, and that was why we were able to slip under it. On the other side of the creek, the bottom of the fence was underwater.

Then I remembered — it seemed like years ago — Todd had shown me the map and said we'd have to go through the proving grounds, where the Army tested weapons. Totally off limits.

"You said you know some kids who go hiking here?" I asked.

"It's perfectly safe, they said. The Army hardly ever uses it."

I jumped in the air, pumping my fists, and slipped on the wet plywood when I came down, yelling, and landing with a wham on my butt. Then I laughed. There was Mr. Harris, yelling something after us, and here we were just gliding away down the creek, easy as you please, passing by a rifle range, and then a burned-out concrete bunker. Just like Huck Finn. Right!

"Todd," I said, "we're miracle workers."

"Unbelievable," he said. "Unbelievable luck."

"No," I said, "it was Ricardo. He's a saint. We've got to get this raft back to him some way."

The sky was dark and bright at the same time. Bright because the clouds were moving away and the storm was completely done, but dark because it was getting toward evening. I realized I'd completely lost track of time, this entire day. Was it morning when I'd met Ricardo? Or noon? I didn't know how long I'd slept both times. It sure hadn't been enough. I was still pumped up, but I knew as soon as I cooled down I could use some more sleep. But since it was almost dark it was time for the final push. We ought to be at Dad's house by morning.

"He knows where we are now, though!" I said to Todd, and I sat up. "He'll call the cops."

"He sure will," said Todd. "We'll have to leave the creek."

"Leave the creek! How will we get to Dad's?"

"I've still got the roadmap," Todd said. "We can use that. We'll have to walk on backroads and try to keep out of sight."

"How did Mr. Harris figure out our route?"

"I don't know." Todd sounded a little mad, the way he had more and more the last day or so. "But I doubt we're the major police priority in the area. I doubt they're putting a round-the-clock guard around Dad's house."

"What if he got off the roof?" I said. "What if he's just sitting in his backyard reading the paper when we get there?"

"That," Todd said, "I doubt very much."

We were floating around a bend in the creek, and Mr. Harris had become a little figure in the distance. For some reason, from far away, he reminded me of Gumby. I watched him finally take his hands off that fence and start to walk away. It was like it took him that long to realize he'd lost us again. It's strange, I thought, how much time and worry he's putting into chasing us. He must really have been thinking about us, and he must know Todd pretty well, I decided, to figure out we'd follow the creek to Dad's place.

And then I had a realization. Major realization. It made my throat feel smaller. It made my stomach bubble, like I'd just eaten fifteen red-hots at once.

"Todd," I said, "do you think Mr. Harris and Mom . . . ?"

"Oh," Todd said, with his don't-you-know-anything voice, "you just figured that out?"

"You mean they're — going together?"

"That's been going on since last winter. That's where she goes when she says she's going shopping."

"Then she's lying to us?"

"I don't know. She hasn't been seeing him that much. Maybe she figured she'd wait until it got more serious before she told us. Except with him coming after us like this — I guess he must really want to impress her."

The raft wasn't spinning, I realized. That meant that my head was. I was suddenly picturing Mom in a wedding dress, standing up at the altar with . . . him? Would he keep on calling me "Buddy"? Would Todd and I have to dress up in starched shirts and ties and be ushers?

"This is too weird," I said. "He's your *teacher!* Teachers and parents aren't supposed to get mixed up!"

"Where'd you read that law? Face it, Worm. Dad's not coming back. Mom's on her own. It's normal she'd want to go out with someone."

Maybe, but I didn't care. I hated her. I hated Mr. Harris. I didn't feel one bit sorry for him now. And I was starting to hate Todd, too.

I said, "I have an idea what we should do when we see Dad."

"An idea?"

"Yes, Todd. I think we should stand on his lawn, and sing that version of the 'Old Mill Stream' song. You know, the one with the funny lines after the serious ones? He'll laugh. That's the first thing he needs to do. Laugh."

"The first thing you need to do is grow up."

"You know, Todd, you would have been in a lot of trouble on this trip without me."

"Dad needs hospitalization. He needs a real doctor looking at him."

"You want to have him committed."

"If you want to put it that way, yeah. He's got serious problems. Face it, Worm! Anyone who sits up on the roof of his house for however many days has got problems! You can't mess around with that."

"Oh, and you're going to tell him to go into the hospital, and he's going to go."

"No. But with Mom helping me . . ."

"Mom is going to kill you when we finally get home."

Todd shook his head. He said, "Being out here in the woods has given me a lot of time to think." My stomach started to worry.

Todd said, "This whole running away business was really stupid. We can't do anything for Dad by ourselves. We need Mom's help. And you know who else's. I was just thinking this right now. Mr. Harris. I mean, he's with Mom. He even teaches two health classes. He might even know which doctor to call for Dad."

I put my hands over my ears and screamed. I counted to ten, and then I looked up. Todd was looking at me like I was a . . . yeah, a you-know-what.

I said, "We're not putting Dad into a mental hospital."

"Whoa!" Todd laughed. "Worm! Sounds like you really got your mind made up on this one."

"I'm not going to see Dad sitting around in pajamas watching TV in the — what do they call it — the day room! In some hospital with a bunch of crazy people!"

"He *is* crazy."

I jumped at him, and shoved him, and before my very eyes he slipped and fell into the creek. I still don't know how I did that. Guess I must have caught him off balance.

Truth is, it felt good.

He swam after the raft, which was moving along very slowly. The creek had spread out wide, in a kind of hollow where hills sloped up from it gradually. Red-clay hills with nothing but honeysuckle tangled up all over them, as if the Army had cut down all the trees there, or maybe blew them up not too long ago.

Todd grabbed hold of the edge of the raft, and tried to drag himself back on with one hand. I think he would have kept trying all night if I hadn't come over and given him a hand. But I didn't go over to him right away. From the look on his face I felt like if I touched him my hand might get burned.

"You thought that was funny?" he hollered. "You know the matches were in my pocket? What exactly are we going to do for a fire now? And the pole's gone! You little moron!" He was going to grab me but I said:

"Don't touch me!" And he didn't. I was amazed. But I felt sick. Sick that Todd and I could even talk to each other like that. And just sad. Deep-down sad, maybe the kind of sad that Dad felt. I just wanted to get off that raft, and I told Todd. The pole was floating right next to us in the water. I fished it out and pushed us over to the shore.

I got off. But first, I grabbed two things from the backpack. The first was the Secret of Marriage. I know, it seemed a little dumb at that point. Like whatever was in that box had some kind of magic. But I'd brought it this far and if I left it behind it would seem like I was turning my back on everything I cared about.

I also grabbed the map from the side pocket and Todd said, "Give me that!" But before he grabbed it back, I looked at what he'd written in big letters and circled, and imprinted it on my brain: MAPLE COURT. *Maple Court*, I whispered to myself, *Maple Court Maple Court . . .*

"Don't be ridiculous, Worm," Todd said. "Get back on the raft. We'll go down a little farther and then strike away from the creek."

Strike away . . . it was such a GI Joe thing to say. It made me wonder if Todd was still playing Army, in some weird way. It made me wonder if he actually would be lonely if I walked away. It made me wonder if I should stay. But only for a second.

I said, "Goodbye."

He looked amazed. I'll never forget that look on his face.

With the Secret of Marriage under my arm, I

walked away from the creek, straight into the honeysuckle.

It was like being swallowed by a huge plant. There were vines in there that grabbed my wrists, and sticky stuff that got all over my face, and a thousand gnats and mosquitoes. The smell smacked me in the face, like a greenhouse on fire. I kicked and swung my arms and finally came staggering out on the other side, sat down for a second, to catch my breath, then jumped up and started to run.

I came to a fence. An enormous fence that had barbed wire on the top. I walked along it, wondering when I was going to run into Lieutenant Colonel BadButt and get hauled away to the clink (or whatever they called it in the Army), and still trying to keep from crying. I almost missed seeing the spot where the bottom of the fence had been curled up a little. But I'm a master at spotting stuff like that, like trails that show where kids cut through backyards, tree forts that are supposed to be secret, milk crates stacked up behind schools for kids to use to climb up on the roof. Even as messed up as I was feeling right then, I still saw the hole. Of course, it was where kids in the neighborhood, when they got old enough and brave enough, snuck into the Proving Grounds. I snuck out.

I had no idea where I was going to go. Maple Court — which way was it? East? Which way was east? It was near the creek, but I couldn't follow the creek. But I knew one thing, and it was burning in my head; I knew I was going to find Dad's house and do *something*, something to help him. I was *not* going to get nailed by the cops or Mr. Harris or Mr. Anybody, not as long as I had two legs to run with.

So I sat down. I tried to make my eyes stiff, so I wouldn't cry. How do you make your eyes stiff? I just felt so lost, and beaten up . . . I felt beaten up inside. Todd and I were partners in this whole thing, and then, just like that, we weren't. So maybe we'd never been. I wondered if he would hate my guts forever, or just for several months. I wanted to know how in the world I was going to find Dad all by myself, not even knowing where I was, and with no money, and nothing to eat, and not even an extra set of clothes. I had to find him fast; I couldn't just sit and think and hide for a day, the way I wanted to. I felt like the sky had fallen and landed on me and I was trying to push it back up again all by myself.

No wise old man came by to say, "What's wearing you down, son?"

Lassie didn't find me and nuzzle me and lead me away on an adventure.

Bees buzzed and cicadas hummed, and it was hot even though it was dark.

And that was it. I said to myself — this is what I said — I said, "Self? What holds up the sun?"

"Sunbeams."

I said, "What happened to the kid who ran away with the circus?"

"They made him bring it back."

I didn't laugh. I was a long way from laughing. But I stood up.

TEN

I found a trail and followed it through pines that seemed to go on forever. Nothing but pine trees. There were little clearings in the trees where I walked past old fire rings and cheap tarps left behind by kids camping out. I crossed a dirt-bike trail, all gouged up by the tires, and in the dark the jump the kids had made looked like a monster with antlers. There were spots where I walked over piles of beer cans from where the high-school kids must have had their parties. It seemed like I was never going to get anywhere, even though I didn't know where I was going. I guess I just wanted a road, or somebody I could ask directions from. The gnats in my eyes made it hard to see. I said:

"There once was a boy and Worm was his name
He said, 'If I get lost won't that be a shame.
I could walk through these pine trees for twenty-
  five miles
Spend the rest of my life wearing upside-down
  smiles.' "

I know, but I was just too deep-down scared to make up a good rhyme. I stopped every few minutes, and looked back to make sure the trail was both in front and behind me. What if the gnats blinded me and I walked off on some other trail that just turned into nothing and I didn't realize it and I ended up standing in the middle of the woods with no trail? What if this was some kind of pine plantation that went on for ten miles in this direction? Should I turn around? Was that traffic I heard up ahead, or a creek? Was I all turned around and headed back to Accomack Creek? That powerful smell of pine trees, kind of like the smell of railroad ties in the sun, was clogging up my head. I kept hearing this buzzing sound, and I'd turn around, thinking someone was behind me with a remote control car, but I was alone. It was like the trees were buzzing.

Finally I heard a sound that I knew was cars. I got

so excited, I started to run. Civilization! But when I came out of the trees, I dropped down and tucked the Secret of Marriage against my stomach and started to crawl. I crawled to the edge of this two-lane highway and lay on my stomach and looked around. I wasn't playing any GI Joe. I was just plain old scared. I was sure Mr. Harris would suddenly drive up in a car and jump out and say, "Let's go!" Or a police car would come screaming up and they'd jump out and handcuff me. I couldn't stand being alone. I wanted to go back and try to find Todd and make up and keep on going together, but unfortunately that was impossible. I just kept repeating to myself: *Maple Court. Maple Court.* But I couldn't move. Cars went by and blew carbon monoxide in my face, and I lay there imagining Maple Court: big cool maple trees, everything damp, like someone had just hosed the street down, Dad's house surrounded by a big green lawn that just turned into his neighbors' lawn with no fences, and kids running around playing with flashlights because it was getting dark. Catching lightning bugs. And their parents sitting out on the steps drinking iced tea.

The only reason I finally moved was that I was dying of thirst. I didn't have money to even buy a root beer, but I walked alongside the trees, a little distance from the highway, figuring I could hide there if the police came along. I thought if I found a gas station, at least I could get a drink from the bathroom.

It felt like the world had ended on that highway. I knew I was near lots of houses but I didn't see any, and hardly any cars came by. Every time I came around a bend I was praying I'd see some kind of lights ahead, even if they were way off in the distance, but no. Just the dark trees, and once in a while a pair of headlights zipping by. The road smelled steamy. I decided there had been a nuclear war. There was a town or a subdivision up ahead, but I couldn't see its lights because it had just been annihilated by a fifteen-megaton warhead. I hadn't heard the blast because it had hit right when I pushed Todd off the raft. I'd been a little distracted.

When I saw a 7-Eleven ahead I started to run. Then I thought I might pass out if I ran, so I settled for walking fast. My arm was all slick from wiping the sweat off my face.

The 7-Eleven was so air-conditioned inside, it felt like Antarctica. No one was in there except an Indian guy. An Indian guy from India, I mean. And maybe it turned out to be a good thing that I was so thirsty and scared. I set the Secret of Marriage down on the counter, and the lies just started spilling out of me — big lies. I didn't know where they came from, except desperation.

"Hi," I said, "our car broke down up the road a

ways and my dad and I decided to split up because we didn't know which way a gas station was, so, could you tell me where the nearest gas station is?"

"Oh — where is your car?"

"About a mile that way."

"Ah — you came the wrong way. Your father will find the gas station. It's about — oh — another half mile past where your car is."

"Great. You know, he forgot to give me any money or anything — and I'm dying of thirst —"

"Of course."

He had a faucet behind the counter, so he filled a mug with water, and then put ice in it. The nectar of the gods. The mug said: MADRAS ATHLETIC CLUB. I drank the whole thing without stopping.

"More?"

"Please."

I finished off the next one, set the mug on the counter, and said in this amazingly cool, just this "oh-by-the-way" kind of voice: "You know what else? We were trying to find Maple Court. And he doesn't have a real good map. Do you know where Maple Court is?"

He was a very nice guy, and the place was empty so he didn't have much else to do. He looked up at the ceiling, stroked his moustache, and said, "Maaa-aaaaple Court . . ." He really reminded me of President Bush. He was an older guy; he had some white in his moustache, and he had that slightly creaky voice, like Bush has, and he was real thin, and he had that little smile that makes you think he's afraid people won't like him. I always thought that was the funniest thing. You can be President, and still have that smile that says: "Oh boy, I hope you'll like me. I hope you won't hate me." That's the smile this guy had.

"Well, my friend," he finally said, "we can look it up." And he walked over to the rack by the door and got one of those Northern Virginia road atlases, the ones that have every single street in all of Fairfax County. I don't know why Todd never got one of those in the first place. "It's near here, no?" he said and I just nodded and hoped it was.

He had to try a few pages, but finally he found it. I couldn't believe how many subdivisions and townhouse developments there were on just a few pages of that atlas. I asked him if I could borrow a pen, and I wrote directions on my left hand. He offered me a piece of scrap paper, but I was afraid I'd lose it. It felt better having it on my skin anyway.

Then I shook his hand. He said, "You're welcome," and then — why? — I bowed. He laughed out loud. Turned out he had a great laugh. "You're very welcome," he said. I felt like an idiot as I walked out. Did I think that was what they did in India? I was just so grateful to the guy. He'd saved my life.

I felt like less of an idiot as I walked along and thought about things. I began to think I might actually make it to Dad's. I got a good look at the maps when the 7-Eleven guy was flipping through them, and it looked like I was even taking a shortcut compared to the way we would have gone if we'd kept following the creek. Plus, I'd be on all little streets through subdivisions, places maybe the police or Mr. Harris wouldn't look. I followed the highway just a little farther, and then I came to a subdivision called Tall Oaks, where all the trees had been cut down when they built the houses, naturally. People who'd bought the houses had planted new trees in the front yards, little spindly ones with wires helping them stand up. I just kept walking, and looking at my left hand every time I came to a streetlight, and making turns when it said to, and praying that I hadn't written anything down wrong.

Now I was glad it was dark. It made me feel safer. But at one point, I was walking down the street that seemed like the main street of Tall Oaks. There were houses all along it, just like the other streets, but the street was wider and the cars went tearing along as if it was the Beltway. Wouldn't you know it, just when I wasn't feeling so scared anymore — here comes a police car right behind me. I jumped onto the lawn beside the sidewalk, and started to crawl. I crawled through the grass and just kept crawling, not even looking back, until I reached the corner of someone's house. Suddenly I realized I was looking at a pair of hairy legs. There was a man attached to the hairy legs. He looked down at me and said, "Can I help you?"

I looked back — no police car in sight. "I guess I just got lost," I said. I stood up, and gave him my dumbest grin, and shrugged, and beat feet back across his lawn and down the street.

Then I saw another police car. I started to wonder if there was a car wreck up ahead. I figured that'd be just my luck. But then I thought it might not be so bad. If there was a serious accident, or better yet, a burglary, why would the police want to bother with me? A fire, I finally decided — I didn't want anybody's house to burn down, but if it was going to anyway, let tonight be the night. That's all I was asking for.

I passed the Tall Oaks Community Swimming Pool, and after a few more blocks, I came to the end of Tall Oaks. But you could only tell because the types of houses changed. These looked like little boxes, instead of big boxes like the ones in Tall Oaks. There were more kids too, still out in the street. I passed some guys playing basketball in their driveway under a big outdoor light and they looked at me; for a second I thought they were going to ask if I wanted to play. "Sorry," I would have said, "got my dad sitting on a roof up ahead here." They didn't ask. Maybe they noticed my boots. I passed a girl going the opposite way from me and she walked off the sidewalk onto the grass to get around me. I thought that was weird for a second and then I wondered what I smelled like. I touched my hair and realized it was probably a little wild. Good thing that 7-Eleven guy didn't call the police when he saw me. Maybe he thought I was in a band.

I passed the Community Park, closed after dark, and another police car passed me. There was a big streetlight there and I looked at my left hand, and I realized I had only two more turns to make to get to Maple Court. This was it. I'd done it. I'd actually done it!

Even though we'd gotten stuck in the mud and had our stuff stolen and gotten chased by Mr. Harris and had nothing to eat and nothing to sleep in and Todd and I had split up and I'd had to do the last bit on my own — the Worm had triumphed! That sounded so good in my head, I said it out loud:

"The Worm has triumphed!"

I should have known.

Guess why I had noticed so many police cars passing me by. Take one guess. There were three police cars next to Dad's house, but their lights weren't flashing. This made me feel better for some reason. The moon was up, and it had turned out to be a pretty bright night, even with the heat-haze still in the sky. I was sneaking through the bushes in the yard across from Dad's house, so I could see Dad sitting up on top of his house. I could see his outline. The house looked big enough for one bedroom and a kitchen you could barely turn around in. There weren't any big maple trees in the yard, either. There weren't any trees at all. It was just a dead-end street with little boxy houses looking at each other from their scraps of grass.

I couldn't even think of what to do, except scrunch down in those bushes and watch. How could I even talk to him with the police there? But I didn't feel scared too long before I started feeling mad. All that way I'd come, for this? Why couldn't I have gotten there before his neighbors finally called the police? What was I going to do now, sit there and watch him get hauled away? And then what? Walk home? Call Mom? Never! No way! But what else?

Then someone climbed out of one of the police cars, lifted a big megaphone to his mouth, and started to talk. And I was so amazed, I stood straight up behind my bush and stared. Thank God it was dark, or they would have seen me in a minute.

It was Todd. For one second — this was how paranoid my brain was getting — I actually wondered if Todd had been on the side of the police all along, and once I'd left he'd somehow called them up and . . . NAAAAAAAAH!

He'd just gotten caught, that's all. Mr. Harris had found him or Mr. Harris had called the police and they'd found him, and now the police had told him to try to talk to his dad.

It was almost funny. Because he didn't need that

big megaphone, he could have just talked loud and Dad would have heard. Dad was only about twenty feet off the ground. It wasn't like he was standing on top of the Brooklyn Bridge or something. But the first thing Todd said amazed me all over again. He said, "Dad! Please throw the knife on the ground! And come down!"

Knife? Dad had a knife? What for? To protect himself? To hurt himself? No. That wasn't possible, and I knew it. They — the police and Todd — had it all wrong. I knew that. I had to get up there and find out.

Todd told him he loved him. That was nice. I don't know if he'd ever said that when Dad wasn't sitting on a house with a knife in his hand.

A ladder. That's all I needed. A ladder, on the other side of the house, where the police wouldn't see. I'd be right up there before they knew what was going on. Dad had always left the ladder on the carport at home. That way, if we came home and didn't have a key, we'd just grab the ladder and climb up and let ourselves in through our bedroom windows.

But he didn't have a carport anymore. And even if he did, it'd be pretty hard to get across the front yard in front of three police cars without being noticed.

I decided there was only one hope. I'd have to become a thief.

I crawled across two yards, heading up the street, until I was sure I was far enough away that the police wouldn't see me. I tucked the Secret of Marriage under my T-shirt, against my back, where it kept slipping down and falling out. My knees were soaked and my hands were covered with grass clippings, those teeny-tiny bits that you can't get off without a hose. I hustled across the street, running bent over double. I had my mind made up.

I was going to do this.

I crawled across two more lawns, coming back down the opposite side of the street, Dad's side. The police and Todd were basically on the far side of Dad's house from me. They were partly in his driveway, so if it was daylight they would have seen me in two seconds. But I felt pretty safe. The neighbors who'd come out to watch were standing right over by the police cars, so as long as no one suddenly came out of one of their houses I figured I was OK. I crawled so close to one house, I could hear the TV. They were watching *Roseanne*.

When I got to Dad's next-door neighbor's house, I crawled into the backyard. See, when I'd been hiding across the street, I'd spotted a tool shed, the kind you buy pre-made at the hardware store, sitting all by itself right in the middle of the neighbor's backyard. I just knew there had to be a ladder in there. All I had to do was sneak over, grab it, and get back over to Dad's house and up on his roof from behind. No sweat!

Unfortunately there was a fence around this particular backyard, and the reason there was a fence around this backyard was, there was a dog in the backyard.

He wasn't a poodle either. I'm not sure what he was, but he looked like he had some German shepherd in there somewhere. He growled at me as I crawled up to the fence. But he didn't bark. He seemed to be waiting to see what I would do.

I got bitten by a dog once, when I was a little kid. It was in a park; I went up to pet the dog and it went wild and chomped me. I still have the scars, but they're all behind my ear fortunately. I think the dog got put to sleep. So you can imagine my inner feelings about dogs; but tonight I was on a roll. Nothing was going to stop me, as long as I only thought about two steps ahead. Thank God, Kenny wasn't there. If he'd heard the next thing I said, he would never have given it a rest.

"Sweet poochy." The dog cocked its head. "I love you, poochy. Nicey-nice doggie. Daddy's dog."

I finally tucked the Secret of Marriage back under my T-shirt and tucked my T-shirt in tight as it would go and crawled over the fence, reaching out my hand, praying the dog would sniff it and not bite it. When he sniffed it, he was still growling. But right then, I knew he wasn't going to hurt me. It was like living in the woods for three days had clued me into animals better. How did I know he was going to be OK? Something about the way he held his body? He had his shoulders back a little. His back legs were set to back up, not to charge. I was paying attention to things like that now, instead of daydreaming about Bugs Bunny or worrying about my bellybutton.

He followed me across the yard, a little ways away, still growling but never barking. I wonder what I said to him. Probably invited him to my birthday party. Carefully — carefully — carefully — I opened the door of that shed. Good thing it wasn't locked. I hadn't even considered that possibility when I'd concocted my careful plan. I could see the glow of a TV through the back window of the house. It seemed to be in a room in the front, though. How could the guy be watching TV when there were three police cars next door, I wondered. It's funny the things you have time to wonder about when you're stealing someone's ladder.

It was even an extension ladder. It was in there behind buckets of paint and a wheelbarrow and a fertilizer spreader and a bunch of shovels and hoes. I wondered what he needed all that stuff for, with a lawn the size of a postage stamp. Maybe he rented a lawn somewhere so he could use all his stuff. Maybe he collected lawn equipment. Oh, I had all kinds of time to think as I went through this guy's shed. It was like I was moving in slow motion. I picked up the wheelbarrow, and set it outside the shed. I figured that would make the least noise. I did the same thing with the spreader and the shovels and the hoes and the paint, and when I was done it looked like this guy was having a tag sale in his backyard. But I had my ladder.

It banged the roof of the shed as I was taking it out. I froze. Even the dog froze. It seemed like the entire world had turned away from their TV's and their megaphones and their phone conversations a mile away to stare at me and the huge noise I'd just made. I might have set a world record for holding breath right there.

But nothing happened. I aimed that ladder straight out the door, even though it was really hard to hold that way, and my arms felt like they were going to drop off from the strain; and I walked step-by-step out of that shed until I was sure nothing, not the back, not the front, not the side, not the rungs, was going to bang.

I held the ladder over my head. Once you get it balanced, it's not so hard. I carried it over to the fence, and tipped it over to get the feet onto Dad's lawn, and set the rest of it on the fence, and climbed over with the dog still growling behind me, a little louder, like there was something he'd forgotten to do and now he was a little mad at himself.

I thanked him. I told him I'd bring him a steak next time I came back, unless he was a vegetarian, in which case I'd bring him some tofu. No, I don't know what I said, probably nothing because now if a policeman was to come around the side of the house I was sunk. I'd be dead, dead meat. I had to move.

I carried the ladder right up to the edge of the house. I'd helped Dad paint our house the summer before, so I knew you had to lay the ladder on the ground with the feet up against the house, and then push the whole thing up against the side, and then position the feet again. I extended it just far enough to reach the gutter, so the police wouldn't see the top of it from the other side of the house. Todd was still talking. He was saying, "Dad, let me come up there. Let me come up there." But as far as I could tell, Dad wasn't saying anything.

I climbed up as quietly as I could until I got about halfway, and then I practically ran up that stupid ladder. Because I figured that at that point, who cared if the police saw me? What were they going to do, shoot me? I was up there. I'd made it. I was on the roof. I was running across the shingles.

ELEVEN

Dad turned, and the knife was in his hand, and for a second I almost fell over backwards. I couldn't see his face, but I knew what he was feeling. I could even smell how he was feeling. He was scared to death. He was ready to jump on someone the same way a cornered dog is ready to jump.

"Willy!" he yelled. "Willy! What are you doing here?"

"I came to help you," I said, and then — well, I'd been thinking about this for three days now and I still didn't know. *Think*, I told myself, think just two steps ahead.

Then the first step seemed pretty obvious. I said, "Can I sit down with you?"

"Of course." He waved me over with the knife.

I crawled up the roof — it was pretty steep and it occurred to me at one point that I could fall, if I wasn't careful, and break my neck — but I got up beside him, and sat down on the peak.

I wanted to hug him, but he smelled too strange, and besides he was still holding that knife between us. It was a kitchen knife, but it was a big one, the kind you use to carve a roast with.

Dad was wearing a yellow raincoat that went down to his knees, and his hair, which he didn't have that much of, was flying all over the place. He looked even skinnier than normal, and taller, too — I don't know how he could be taller, except that being up on a roof just made him look taller.

"Get off of there!" someone yelled from down below, and I heard Todd shout, "Worm, you don't know what you're doing!" I didn't know what to say to them so I turned to Dad and said:

"How are you?"

He laughed and said, "I've been OK. Really, Willy. I do have a few problems now . . . it seems they want to send me to the nuthouse." He pointed at the police below. "There's no point in that. But your brother is very insistent."

"How come they don't just come up here and get you?"

He laughed very loud — not his real laugh. "They seem to think I'm a danger to myself and others, because of this!" He raised the knife up over his head, and you could hear everyone below go: "Aaaaaaaaaaaaaah!" Did they think he was going to chop off my head?

"It's the funniest thing," Dad said. "I was in a hurry when I came up here. I mean, it just came to me one day that I needed to sit up on the roof for a while. Right away. So I grabbed a jar of peanut butter and a jar of jelly and a loaf of bread, for provisions, and I realized as I was rushing out the door that I'd need a knife. So I grabbed the nearest one, even though it wasn't the most appropriate. Now everyone thinks I've armed myself!" He stuck the knife up toward the sky again, and you could feel a big shudder down below, and Dad said, "It's the silliest thing."

"Did Todd tell you how we got here?"

"Yes, he did, and I must say I'm terribly proud of you." He reached over with his free arm and hugged me, and I snuggled up against his side, and he stopped smelling strange. I felt safe, and I hadn't felt safe for three days. I said, "Did Todd tell you I learned to snare squirrels?"

"No! Our conversation didn't get very far, as you might guess. The first thing he said was he wanted me to go to an institution."

I told Dad about the squirrels, and about the raft and Mr. Harris and Ricardo and the whole adventure, and he especially wanted to hear about what I did after Todd and I split up. He said that struck him as the bravest thing of all, to just keep on going after I was all by myself. I said:

"Are you being brave up here?"

"I wouldn't call this bravery," he said. "I'd call this desperation."

"What exactly happened?"

"Nothing. That's just it. I didn't find a new job. I didn't feel better. I didn't see any chance that your mother wanted to get back together. I mean, I don't want to drag you into all my ups and downs, Will, but I just thought I needed some time to get my head together. It seemed very urgent. I suppose I could have driven out to the Shenandoah or something and no one would have thought twice about it, but this roof seemed much more convenient and accessible. My mistake! Not the first one, or the last —"

"But where do you go to the bathroom?"

"For number one," he said in a pretend whisper, "I go over the side. For number two, I sneak down my ladder and go back in the house. But they took down my ladder, for some reason."

"But where do you get a drink?"

"There's a water bottle tied around the vent-stack over there," he said. "And if I'm feeling lazy, I squirt myself in the mouth with my trusty water pistol here." He patted his pocket. "Do you want to know how I sleep?"

I nodded.

"There's another rope around the vent-stack that I tie around my waist. And then I get into my sleeping bag. I'm like a rock climber up on my roof! Suspended in the heavens!"

"Do you really sleep?"

"I must confess, Will, even for me, five days without a break would have been a bit much. No, the first few nights I went down and slept in my warm bed. I even made myself bacon and eggs one morning. But these last few nights I've been pretty comfortable, surrendering myself to the strength of my vent-stack each night." I looked at it. It was just a little metal pipe that stuck up through the roof, with a round metal cap on top.

I said, "So you didn't spend five straight days up here?"

"Don't tell a soul."

"You got it." It messed up the story, after all, if he hadn't been up there straight through. And naturally, being me, I never completely stopped thinking about the story I'd tell my friends when this was all over.

"This has been a good experience for me, though," said Dad. "It got me out of bed, first of all! Did you know I spent the five days previous to this basically in bed? Now that's depression! And yet, would the police come and camp outside my house because I was in bed for five days? Oh well. At least I've come to some conclusions. One is, I've got to start calling everyone I know about finding work. I mean, that's how you do it. Through people. And two is, I need to talk to more people anyway. I've got to stop hiding myself away. And three is, I've got to talk to your mother about solidifying our arrangements for sharing you. You and Todd. That's what scares me, when I think about the way I've been acting. It scares me that I haven't been seeing you. Why did I let that happen?"

"Mom's scared, too."

"So many people are afraid of me!" He laughed that barking kind of laugh again. "It's so comical! Me!"

"Dad —"

"The terror of Maple Court!"

"Dad —"

"The only person I usually scare is myself, when I look in the mirror."

"*Dad!* Someone's coming up that ladder!"

He turned in time to see a policeman's face rise up above the edge of the roof. "Now take it easy, friend," said the policeman. "I'm coming up there."

"Fine!" Dad shouted. "Let's chat!"

"That's right, let's chat," said the policeman.

"I'll make you a sandwich," Dad said, and once again he whipped that knife up in the air. When the policeman got a leg up on the roof, I could see clear as daylight that he had a gun on his hip. Then I heard a noise from behind me.

Another ladder — we were under attack! I couldn't think what their plan was, unless the first policeman was supposed to distract Dad while the second one snuck up on him. Fat chance. Maybe, I thought, they were planning to rush us once they got close enough. Then I saw Todd's face rise up from under the edge of the roof. I couldn't see his face real well, but I knew it was him. I said, "Hi."

"The cops came right onto the Proving Grounds. Maybe fifteen minutes after you went. I didn't think they'd do that."

"No kidding. I just walked here. This guy in a 7-Eleven showed me a map."

"No kidding," Todd said.

"Todd!" Dad cried. "Wonderful! If only I had a deck of cards!"

The weirder things get, the sillier Dad gets. You should have seen him right before Mom asked him to leave the house.

The policeman said, "It sounds like you're feeling very scared about this commitment business."

"Don't try your reflective listening on me!" Dad shouted. "Listen, what kind of sandwich do you want? P.B. and J. or P.B. and J?" He rummaged around inside his bag, pulled out the bread, and got some slices spread on the shingles, all with one hand, the whole time waving that knife in the air with the other.

"Dad!" I said. "Put the knife down!"

"Oh, don't be silly," he said. "I'm making sandwiches for our guest. We wouldn't want to be poor hosts now, would we? Would you like a drink, Will?" Then he pulled that water gun out of his pocket. It was the kind they make that's supposed to look just like the real thing: this one was a Tech 9. He pointed it at my face and said, "Open wide!" I saw that policeman's hand touch his gun. I made a grab for the water pistol.

He was so surprised, he didn't even hold on to it. I just snatched the water gun out of his hand. But I had to throw myself across him to get hold of it, and sandwiches got mashed all over my Wolverine shirt. He dropped the knife, too, because he was trying to balance himself and keep us from sliding down the roof and the only way he could do that was to grab hold of the shingles with both hands. I started to roll. He reached down and grabbed my Wolverine shirt. He dug his feet against the shingles and the Secret of Marriage slipped out and I grabbed that and Dad pulled on my shirt and I slapped one hand on the roof and the asphalt ground into my skin. Dad dragged me and the asphalt scraped my knees. The policeman was scrambling up the roof and

Todd was coming from the other side and people down below were screaming. One of them sounded like Mom.

If you get momentum going, it can sort of press your feet against a surface and keep you from falling. I learned this when Dad jerked me toward the peak of the roof and I got my feet under me and I started to run, squeezing the Secret with one hand. I met the policeman at the peak of the roof and I said:

"STOP!"

He did.

Then, because I was talking to a policeman, I said:

"OK?"

Dad was climbing up behind me and Todd had his arm. I said to the policeman, "We need to talk. Dad's not coming down off this roof right now unless you drag him and I really don't think you want to try to drag him off this roof because he's going to fight. But if you wait and let us talk, it'll be better."

The policeman was a young guy who was trying to grow a moustache. But it was just a little blond moustache. You could barely see it. I said:

"It's a steep roof."

"OK!" he hollered. "Fifteen minutes." He held up his fingers on one hand, three times, just to make sure I got the point.

I turned around and there were Dad and Todd, staring at me. I said, "Want to go over there?"

I looked down and there was Mom, with her face so white I swear it glowed in the dark. I waved. I said, "We're OK, Mom!"

Todd and Dad were still standing there, so I led them along the peak of the roof down to the vent-stack. They followed. When I sat down, they sat down.

AND THEN —

Well, I had brought that box all the way here from home I guess so I could use it right now. I held it up like I was hoping it might start to glow or something, and Dad said, "Why did you bring that all the way here?"

I said, "I wanted you to open it."

"Oh," he said. Just like that: "Oh." Like I'd just explained everything and of course it made perfect sense. God, I loved him for that. He just took it, and opened it up, like we were sitting at home in the kitchen with the smell of Mom's celery-stock in the air. He got his thumb under the lip of the lid, and pushed up, and the tape ripped, and he pulled out what was inside.

It was round, and gray, and it had a hole in the middle. I crouched down so I could get a better look at it in the dark.

"Listen," called the policeman. "Twelve minutes!"

"We have opened the box!" I yelled. "Stand by!"

I crouched back down again, and touched the little round gray thing. It had a kind of skin on it, made of dust. I touched my fingertip to my tongue, and it tasted like maybe it used to be mold, but now it was only dust.

I whispered, "Is it a doughnut?"

"Is it some kind of herb?" Todd said.

"No," said Dad. He was holding it with two fingers, and smiling like it was a real hard work for him to smile. "It's not an herb, or a doughnut."

"Is it food?" I said.

"It was, originally, a form of food."

"Is it a bagel?" Todd said.

"Yes," Dad said, "it's a bagel." He sighed, and said, "Would you like to hear the story behind it?"

"Yes," I said. I stood up again. I called to the policeman: "My Dad's going to tell us a story! Just hold on till it's over, OK? Don't tell us every three minutes how much time we have, OK?"

The policeman didn't say a word. The three of us were crouched together by the vent-stack, with Dad's sleeping bag rolled up between us. He set the old bagel on the rolled-up bag.

My stomach didn't have to be a genius to know something was coming that I wasn't going to like. And it was telling me.

Dad sighed, and said, "OK. When I was twenty-five years old — I came down here to Virginia to go to graduate school. Now this was after I'd dropped out of a couple of programs in New York. And the reason I dropped out was — I couldn't get out of bed, too many mornings. Or the professor would call on me in class, and I wouldn't hear, even though he called my name five times. Or I couldn't stand the paint being chipped on the classroom doorway."

I said, "I hate chipped paint."

"But I thought maybe a new state would be the charm. And it certainly seemed that way at first. I got to Charlottesville for the spring semester, and spring on that campus was like nothing I'd ever seen. Dogwoods were blooming everywhere, and magnolia trees, everywhere, and the lawns were so bright green I felt like I had to hide my eyes, some mornings. Classes were going well. At first.

"But then, that old feeling started to come back again. The blanket, is how I used to think of it. It was like I was walking around all day with a big wool blanket over my head. And when I woke up in the morning, the blanket felt so heavy that it was a struggle to get out of bed again. I made it through spring semester OK. I took classes in the summer because I thought I could keep myself going that way. But the heat! You know what it's like because you grew up here, but I'd never felt anything like the heat that summer. I felt like I couldn't breathe that air. It was like walking around at the bottom of a pond all day. And even at night the air in my room was like syrup. That made the blanket even heavier, and it got to where I had all these tricks I used to get through the day. I had to have a sixteen-ounce glass of cold orange juice every morning. I had to wear a white shirt to class every day. I couldn't take my slippers off, from the time I woke up until the time I went to bed, so I wore them to class. And whenever I began to feel like I was about to stop — see, that's what I was scared of — that I'd sit down somewhere one day, and not be able to stand up again — whenever I began to feel that way, I'd hum the opening theme of Mussorgsky's *Pictures at an Exhibition.* It had power, somehow."

"Yeah," I said. "I sing the Lone Ranger song when I feel like that." But Dad had his head down like he had to charge through this story. Like if he looked up, he might quit.

"But — bagels. Since I came from the Big Apple, I naturally had a great love for a good bagel, and I mean a *good* bagel, not the bland imitations you generally find everywhere outside New York. When I first came to Charlottesville I searched and I searched for a decent bagel, and at last, I discovered a miracle. A little bakery that made bagels, not quite up to the standards of Third Avenue, but surprisingly close. Dense, chewy, with that certain tangy aftertaste that a good bagel allows. It turned out, of course, that the owner had grown up on the Lower East Side. So, needless to say, one of my necessary routines was to visit this particular bakery every morning."

My stomach was shouting warnings at me now. I

started to ask Dad something about the actual recipe for making bagels, but Todd stuck his toe against my butt, and I shut up. We were sitting in a line on the peak of the roof now, staring out across all the cars and people and flashlights in Dad's front yard. The moon behind the haze in the sky made the haze bright gray.

"The same young woman always worked behind the counter at this bakery. An attractive brunette, about five foot three, with eyes of different colors."

"You met Mom at a bakery?"

Dad nodded. "She was half the reason I went there every day. If I'd been well, I would have asked her out after oh, maybe my third visit. Still, visits to the bakery were one of the things that got me out of bed every morning. So I felt betrayed, I guess — yes, betrayed! — when I stared at the round bagel one morning, on its round paper plate, and the entire room began to swirl around the hole in the bagel. The hole in the bagel was the center of a whirlpool. I couldn't stop staring at it. It wasn't unpleasant. I sort of knew that it wasn't good, to be staring so long. I had no concept that I'd been staring at it for half an hour when your mother tapped me on the shoulder. The tapping felt like a mosquito bite. It hurt, but very faintly. I think the ambulance came after an hour. I honestly don't remember much except the whirlpool. The thing I remember most is that when I came back to the world again, in the hospital, and understood what had happened. I felt betrayed by the bagel. Yes, the bagel had let me down. Isn't that crazy?"

Now I felt like I'd swallowed a bird. I wanted to jump off that stupid roof. But Dad kept talking:

"And I was wrong. It turned out that bagel was the best thing that ever happened to me. It got me into that hospital, and the electric-shock treatments brought me out of my depression, because that's what it was, physical depression, and the doctors were very helpful, too. And not only that, someone brought me my bagel, after I'd begun to recover."

Dad got the biggest, goofiest grin on his face right then. But I turned away, and looked out at the moon-haze.

"Mom," Todd said quietly.

"That's how your mother and I started going out. She was such a good soul, she came to the hospital one day and said, 'You never finished your bagel, sir.' Oh, it was so good to start a relationship with such a good laugh! And this is it, of course." He was waving that hunk of mold around. "This is the very bagel. I saved it all these years, and I thank you, Will, for bringing it here now."

"You never told us you were crazy," I said. I didn't try to say it mad — but from the way Dad looked at me, I knew how it sounded. He put his hand on my shoulder, and said:

"I got sick. Think of it as — I don't know,

malaria. It's something that you get, and it has a way of coming back. But it can be dealt with. Lately, I haven't been dealing with it. I don't need to go back to any hospital now. That's why I've been giving the police such a hard time. Maybe I need to see a doctor, or start taking some kind of medication, or get shock treatments again if I absolutely have to. I think I'll start by seeing a shrink. When you're sick, you ought to go see the doctor."

I scootched my butt down along the peak of the roof, so his hand would fall off my shoulder.

"I didn't want to tell you until I thought you'd be old enough to understand, Will."

"I do understand," I whispered. I think it might almost have been better if I'd yelled it.

"Look, Will," he said after a moment. "I am still the same old person. Fully capable of letting you down sometimes, and I'm sorry. But still always here. Which I'm going to show you right now. All right? I'm going to show you. Are you watching?"

Of course I was. But I wasn't going to turn my head and let him know that.

He said to Todd, "Are you OK?" and I guess Todd nodded because they both went climbing down the other side, and Dad said something to the cops about how they'd have no case in court, that he was not a danger to himself or others, so they could do what they damn well pleased, and then I heard him call me. When I looked up, I saw him waiting for me, at the edge of the roof, with his hand stretched out. Too far away to see the look in his eyes.

Where was that bagel? Hiding? I looked around and spotted it stuck between the vent-stack and the sleeping bag. I grabbed it and gave it a look that could have scorched paint off a wall, and told it, "I should have thrown you in the creek the first day!" I squeezed it and would have hurled it into the darkness right then — but the bagel said, "He needed help, Worm."

I wasn't going to take that from a bagel. I said, "He lied to us! Everything we ever did together was a lie. He took us out to that drive-in in West Virginia, and he played soccer with me even though he hates sports, and he sat by the Beltway with us. All that. And the whole time, he was a person who was once in a straitjacket with electrodes stuck on his head, flopping around like a fish out of water! Illness, my foot! I saw a documentary about it on PBS! He was nuts! Once a nut, always a nut! My father, the mental case!"

"He was sick," said the bagel.

"Here's what I'll say to him, after he comes back from the hospital this time. I'll say, 'Welcome back, Dad! I stuck my finger in this socket here, just to make you feel right at home! Hey, we've been thinking about you. Took a lot of shopping to find square plates!' I'll say, 'What do they call that new cologne you're wearing — Scorch?'"

Then I heard Dad's voice — loud, mad, not like him. "Leave him be! He'll come down when he wants to!" Who was he yelling at? There were a lot of voices down on the driveway. He could have been yelling at the police. Or Mom. Or Todd.

Dad was the only one who would know that I needed to be up there by myself.

"Are you OK, Will?" he called to me. "You're awfully quiet."

I looked at the bagel. I couldn't see how you could sit in a restaurant and stare at it for an hour. It didn't look like a whirlpool to me. It didn't really talk. It just seemed like it should have.

Then I took a little bite out of that bagel. I closed my eyes — which was scary that high off the ground — and I thought I could taste the coffee that sat in Dad's mouth while he stared like a zombie at a stupid bagel in a restaurant, and feel the cold electrodes on his head, and smell the bleach in the sheets on his bed in the hospital. The bagel tasted like dead flies mixed with ashes. Maybe worse. But after awhile, after I held it on my tongue awhile, and my mouth got used to it, and my spit sort of covered it over, I could swallow it. I'm the kind of person who can swallow all kinds of things. I guess I'm sort of known for it.

Dad was still waiting. The way I knew he would be. I stuck the bagel in my pocket, and when I stood up, he reached his hand out again.

He went down first, and I stood up at the edge of the roof for a second. There was a breeze starting up. Way off in the distance, I could see a big dark blob that must have been a clump of trees. I looked down, and all these faces were looking up at me. A bunch of Dad's neighbors, and two policemen, and Todd, and Dad, and Mom, and Mr. Harris. She was standing so close to Mr. Harris, their hips must have been touching. But I wasn't surprised. Since they were all looking at me, I figured I might as well say something.

I said, "Hello."

I climbed down the ladder, and man, my feet felt good on that grass. It's funny how you don't even know how nervous your body gets about being up high until you touch the ground again. The sweet solid ground. Mom hugged me. I waved to Mr. Harris, and he nodded back. Todd shook my hand. He looked back at Dad, so I knew he and Dad had been talking about something. Then I knew what it was, when he said:

"Do you want me to start calling you Will?"

"No," I said, just like I'd had a long time to think about it. But I didn't need to think about it. It was Worm who'd tromped through the rain, and snared squirrels, and found his way here, and Worm who could maybe start thinking, one of these days, real late at night maybe if he couldn't sleep, about his father having been in a mental hospital and his mother having a boyfriend. It was Worm who'd come down off the roof, at least. "No thanks," I said. "You can call me Worm."

"OK," Todd said. "OK, Worm."

"And by the way," I said. "The man was riding a horse named Friday."

"Huh?" Todd said, and Dad and Todd and Mom and Mr. Harris and I all walked past the policemen and leaned against Dad's car, to talk.